NATURAL BORN WITCH

WITCHES OF PALMETTO POINT BOOK 8

WENDY WANG

CHAPTER 1

C harlie Payne walked through the doors of the Defenders of Light, and the scent of sage and lavender permeating the air smacked her in the face. She glanced around at the crowds of other people, other witches filing into the building, and realized she'd overdressed for her first day of work. Next time she'd ditch the pant suit and silk blouse and go with the casual jeans like some of the other women wore, pin her blonde hair up in a messy bun. Wearing it down as she had today meant always pushing it behind her ears to keep it from falling in her eyes.

The witches, each sporting a look as individual as Charlie would expect of the DOL staff, Goth black on one, natural fibers and homespun skirts and shawls on another, and even soccer mom jeans and T-shirts on others, swiped their badges to enter the elevator and disappeared inside when the doors opened.

The lobby with its corporate décor looked like every other modern building she'd seen. Except for the smell in the air, that distinct herbal scent, stronger than the last time she'd come here with Ben Sutton, her friend and DOL Agent.

On her last visit, Gerald, the head of security, had told her that lots of nasty creatures came into this building, and they regularly pumped sage and lavender through the heating and air conditioning systems to cleanse the place. She wondered what had come through recently that required such a strong dose of sage? Maybe **just** an overabundance of caution. She wasn't the only new hire starting today, or so Ben had told her. Maybe it was because of them. No one wanted a stray spirit following the new hires into this sacred space.

Charlie noticed a man with blond hair enter the building. Like her, he stopped to take a look around. His nostrils opened, and his chest puffed out, making it apparent he was breathing in the air. Just like her. Maybe he was new here, too. She chanced letting him notice her smiling at him. She'd like to have a compatriot on her first day.

He looked fortyish, older than her by maybe a decade. And he was tall. At least six-two. His pale skin made her question whether he might be a spirit, but Ben Sutton walked through the door and spoke to him, relinquishing any doubt that he might not be alive. Ben's gaze shifted to her, and he smiled widely. He'd shaved his beard, revealing his handsome baby-face. His blue eyes glittered when he waved. She certainly understood why her cousin Jen had fallen so hard for him. Charlie waved back and headed over.

"Hey," she said.

"Hey, Charlie," Ben said. "I'd like you to meet a good friend of mine. Will Tucker, this is Charlie Payne. She's my girlfriend's cousin and a very good friend."

"Nice to meet you," Will said with a distinct twang that Charlie didn't recognize.

"Where're you from, Will?" Charlie asked.

"You ever hear of Solomon's Beach, Florida?" he asked.

"No, I'm afraid not," Charlie said.

He laughed. The warm sound of it wrapped around her. "Nobody ever has, I guess. It's on the panhandle of Florida, near the Alabama border."

"Oh." Charlie nodded politely at that. She noticed a pale scar skirting along the line of his jaw. It was an old scar by the look of it, faded and stretched thin as if he'd grown into it. No hair grew there that she could see. She imagined that if he had kept a beard like Ben used to, or scruff like Jason sometimes did, that it would look like a line in the sand, or in the hair. He scratched his jaw, obscuring the scar and gave her a sideways glance. Charlie's cheeks heated and she looked away.

"Have you picked up your badge yet?" Ben asked.

"No," Charlie said.

"Come on." Ben gestured for them to follow him and took a few steps toward the security desk near the elevators. "I want to get all this admin stuff out of the way fast. We've picked up an interesting case that I want both of you to see."

Charlie moved first, but Will quickly caught up with her, his long legs keeping stride.

"What's the case?" Charlie asked.

"A missing family of witches," Ben said. "Looks like there could be some demonic activity. You both have experience dealing with demons. Not everyone on the team does."

"A demon." Will placed his hand on top of a weathered leather bag that he wore across his body. "I had no idea this job would be so much fun."

"Oh yeah, it's a regular day at Disney around here," Ben quipped.

Will chuckled. Charlie couldn't do much more than nod. Demons were no joke to her, especially considering that one had once kidnapped her cousin Lisa. Charlie couldn't bear the thought of what might have happened if she and her other cousins, Jen and Daphne, together with

Lisa's boyfriend Deputy Sheriff Jason Tate, hadn't found her in time.

The three of them stopped in front of security. A man Charlie had met on her first visit grinned and cocked his head.

"I figured you'd be back," the man said. His graying short hair and silvery mustache were the only things on Gerald Handley's face that gave away his age. His dark skin glistened a little in the natural lighting of the lobby. "Good to see you Miss Charlie."

"Good to see you too, Gerald," Charlie said.

"I need to head upstairs now, but you stop by and see me anytime," Gerald offered. Miss Athena here will take care of you."

"Thank you. I will," Charlie said.

A YOUNG WOMAN CHARLIE HAD SEEN BEFORE SAT BEHIND the desk. Her red curls cascaded down her back, but she'd twisted strands of hair away from her face on each side at her temples and fastened them in place with two barrettes. A bold splay of freckles dotted her cheeks and nose, and her green eyes glinted with good humor when she smiled.

"Hey Athena," Ben said. "These two are starting work today. Can you get them set up, please?"

"Of course." Athena stood up and gestured for them to follow her.

"Hey, Charlie," Ben called before departing. "I'll see you upstairs."

Charlie waved and gave him a reassuring smile.

"You too, Will," Ben said.

Will brought his hand up and gave Ben a loose salute. "See ya, boss."

Athena led them to an office tucked away in the corner of the lobby.

"We just have some paperwork for you to fill out," she said. "And then we'll take your photos, and you can head up to the third floor to meet with HR for your orientation."

"Great," Charlie said, trying to get just the right amount of enthusiasm to show in her voice. Too much and she might sound over-eager, which she didn't want because, if she was honest with herself, she still wasn't sure this had been the best choice for her. Only time would tell.

Charlie took her forms and sat on one side of a small table with two seats. She dug into her purse for a pen and started to fill out the W-4 tax form.

Will didn't say much. He took the forms and sat down at the table across from Charlie. He patted his chest and then his hips as if he were looking for a pen. When he found none, he leaned over, his arm covering part of the form.

"You wouldn't happen to have an extra, would you?" He pointed at her pen.

"Sure," Charlie said. She dug through her purse again for another pen and took out her wallet for the ID she needed for the I-9 form.

"Time's up," Athena crowed.

Charlie and Will both turned their heads with bewildered glares on their faces. Athena chuckled, her green eyes glittering. "Just kidding. Take all the time you need."

"Thanks," Charlie muttered. When they were done with the forms, Athena had them stand in front of a blue background and she took their pictures and laminated the thumbnails onto a 2x3 plastic badge with a ring and a lanyard for hanging around their necks. Charlie inspected her photo and frowned. Her face looked too round for her liking. Had she gained weight? Her boyfriend Tom had been cooking for her nearly every night these past few weeks. Sometimes sumptuous meals and most times with dessert. He made a killer mocha crème brûlée which rivaled her love for her cousin Jen's peach cobbler. None of her clothes felt too tight, but still. Maybe she needed to cut back on the desserts. Will peeked over her shoulder.

"Looks good. Better'n mine." He held up his badge. The acronym DOL glared back at her.

"Yours does too," she said.

He grinned politely, but his eyes told another story. A story of disbelief. He was pretty handsome with his windswept, sandy hair, splay of freckles across his nose, and crystal blue eyes. Did that scar on his face really bother him that much? It was a bit jagged on the ends as if he'd never had it stitched up, but it was so pale and faded.

He slipped the lanyard over his head and let the badge fall to the middle of his chest, the photo of him facing his shirt.

"I'm going to drop you all off at HR to finish up your intro to the company and to pick up your handbooks. Then, either Ben or I will swing by after to show you to the fifth floor," Athena said.

"Great," Charlie said. Her voice sounded too chipper in her ears, and she grimaced a little.

"Cool," Will said.

The two of them followed her into the elevator and to the third floor. It only took half an hour to fill out some more forms, and pick up the passcode encrypted thumb drives with all the company policies on it. It was more high tech than Charlie expected, but she was glad they hadn't mowed down a forest to give out monstrous handbooks.

Ben met them at the door and led them to the fifth floor to a familiar conference room. The wall length whiteboard covering one side of the room no longer held pictures of missing kids from the last case she'd worked on with the DOL. It had been wiped clean and was ready for the next case. Charlie took a seat at the far end of the table facing the door, and Will took the chair next to her.

"I'll be right back," Ben said. "Let me go round up the rest of the team."

Charlie and Will traded uncertain glances. Ben closed the conference room door behind him when he left.

Will tapped his fingers on the heavy wood table, and Charlie could see a slight tremor to one side of his body as if he were shaking his leg.

"Nervous?" she asked, letting her lips form a reassuring smile.

Will let out a breathy laugh. "A little. I've never really worked with a big team of people before. But my partner was killed six months ago, and I, uh..." His face deflated as if the memory had punctured a fresh hole in it.

"I'm so sorry for your loss." Charlie reached across the table and placed her hand on top of one of his, bracing herself for what she might see.

A jumble of dark rooms with moonlight streaming through them flashed through her head. A hissing screech that made all the hair on her arms and neck stand up echoed through her head. A scream and the glimmer of pointed white canines made her jerk her hand back.

Will stared at her. His lips drew up into a thick pink oval.

"Ben said you were psychic," Will said.

Charlie let out a nervous chuckle.

"Yeah," she said.

"You all right?" he asked.

"Yeah." She forced a smile. "The question is, are you all right? I see things sometimes when I touch people."

"Right." He drew his hands off the table into his lap and leaned back in his chair. His gaze shifted away from Charlie's face, staring at the blank whiteboard. "What did you see?"

"It didn't make a lot of sense, but I know I definitely saw teeth. Vampire teeth. Are you a—?"

"You think I'm a vampire?" He sounded half-amused, half- flabbergasted at the suggestion.

"I don't know what I think. I just—"

"I am definitely not a vampire." He laced his fingers together and laid his joined hands on the table. It looked as if he might bow his head and say a prayer at any moment.

"Right," Charlie said, feeling stupid for even suggesting it. "You're a vampire hunter."

A smile lifted the corners of his mouth, and he gave her a le-eyed glance. "Yep. I mean, I hunt lots of things. Dee   juirre'   'e occasional ghost, but mainly vam

"Is that how you got the scar on your face?" She asked the question and immediately wished she could take it back.

His fingers tightened, causing his knuckles to go white.

A strong scent of lavender wafted through Charlie's senses, and she breathed it in. "Do you smell that?"

Will sniffed deeply. "Yep. Ben said they pump sage and lavender through the vents throughout the day."

"I know, but just now it seemed stronger," she said.

"That's because it is. Anytime there are more than four people in a room, extra lavender is pumped in to help with stress levels," Ben said from the doorway. He stepped back and gestured for the group behind him to enter the conference room. Charlie didn't recognize all of the faces. When she saw Darius Fowler and his sister Tomeka Fowler enter the room, Charlie grinned and waved. She touched the chair next to her, pulling it out a little for Tomeka to take a seat. Darius took the next chair. He leaned forward and looked around his sister, his dark brown eyes shined.

"Hey, Charlie," he said.

"Hey, Darius," Charlie said, unable to contain her happiness to see them. "I didn't expect y'all to be here."

"I'm mainly here as a consultant. I still have a business to run so I'm not full time," Darius said. "But Tomeka is."

Charlie clapped her hands together softly. "Yay."

Tomeka ducked her head and grinned.

"Why didn't you tell me?" Charlie asked.

"I wasn't sure I got the job until yesterday when Ben called me," Tomeka said. "It was Darius's idea to keep it a surprise."

"It is a surprise. A very happy surprise, that's for sure." Charlie beamed. She sat back and looked around the table at the others. She recognized the DOL witch Athena from the Keeley Moore abduction case she'd worked on with the DOL's help just a couple of weeks ago. It seemed like forever had passed between then and now. So many changes since then. It made Charlie's head spin when she thought about them all.

The other faces looked familiar, but she couldn't remember their names.

"All right, everyone," Ben said. He closed the door and turned to the table full of people. "First, I want to say welcome to my team. Some of you, like Darius and Marigold," Ben gestured to Darius and a pretty brunette witch with olive skin and dark brown eyes sitting next to Athena, "will only be working with us part-time on a consultation basis, but I wanted to make sure everyone here knew names and faces. I also wanted to help you understand, working with the Defenders of Light means you are considered special. Lauren is pretty picky about approving new hires. What we do here is important, and that means you're important."

His gaze drifted from face to face around the table, pausing just long enough to make eye contact, and to drive home his point. "Why don't we start here?" Ben gestured to the brunette witch he'd called Marigold in the chair nearest him at the end of the table..

"Hi, I'm Marigold Burris. I've worked at the DOL for five years. Ben and I have worked several cases together. Like he said, I'm really only working with this group part-time, but I'm excited about the opportunity." She smiled, finishing up, but Ben said, "And?" followed by a look.

"Oh, and I'm a sea witch," she added.

"Like Ursula from the Little Mermaid?" Charlie gave the young woman a quizzical look. Marigold's eyes widened and she sat up straight in her chair.

"Oh. Uh...not exactly. I'm able to affect the weather and the tides. Most of my craft is done by the light of the moon." Marigold looked to Ben and he gave her a nod of approval before he continued around the circle.

"Hi, I'm Athena Whitley. I've been with the DOL for three years, and I'm excited to be working cases with Ben and this team. Investigative work is a little new to me, so I'm really excited. I'm a green witch with clairvoyance." Her red curls bounced when she spoke, and her pretty freckled face lit up.

Ben pointed to the DOL witch sitting next to Athena.

"I am Sabine Khouri." Her dark brown eyes glistened with excitement, but her deep sultry voice stayed steady. "And I am an elemental witch. I've worked with the DOL for the last four years, and before that, I was part of the International Coalition of Witches."

Will sat up straight in his chair when it was his turn to speak. "Will Tucker. New here. Vampire hunter for the most part." He slumped down in his chair again when he finished and folded his hands in front of him on the table.

"And a man of few words," Ben quipped. Everyone laughed, even Will, but his pale face reddened.

"Yep," Will added.

Ben turned his attention to Charlie. A thrill went through her when everyone turned their gaze on her and she forced a smile.

"Charlie Payne. Like Will, I'm new here. I'm psychic and a witch, but I don't really have a specialty."

"You see the dead, Charlie," Ben reminded her. "And you also have outside investigative experience that's pretty valuable."

Charlie's cheeks heated. "Thanks."

He gave her a nod and a wink, then moved on to Tomeka.

"I'm Tomeka Fowler. I'm clairvoyant, and I read tarot, and um..." Tomeka's dark eyes widened. Charlie sensed her anxiety at being under such intense scrutiny by these people she didn't know.

"You practice hoodoo," Darius chimed in.

"Right, hoodoo," Tomeka said. "Which our grandmother taught us." Tomeka sat back in her chair and looked to her brother.

"Thanks, Tomeka," Ben said. He gave her a reassuring smile.

Darius lifted one of his hands from the table and gave a short wave. "I'm Darius Fowler, Tomeka's brother. I'll only be working with y'all part-time, but it seems like a good group, and I'm excited. I'm an acupuncturist and herbalist by trade. My specialty is necromancy. I've studied many different cultures, including Chinese, which I incorporate into my craft, as well as the traditional hoodoo my family practices." He smiled, and a sense of calm spread across the room. Tomeka visibly relaxed, and the flutter in Charlie's belly quelled. One of these days, she would have to ask him how he did that.

"Great, thanks. You all know who I am," Ben started, "and, like you, I'm excited about this team. I think we've got a tremendous opportunity to do some real good in the world, and I'm really happy you all are here."

Charlie chanced a peek at Will. His stoic angular face reminded Charlie of a general carved in marble. He didn't give off much emotion that she could sense. And maybe that was a good thing.

Ben clapped his hands, then rubbed them together. "Now that we all know each other, who's ready to hear about our first case?"

Everyone's hand shot into the air.

"Great, let's begin."

CHAPTER 2

Ben opened the folder he'd brought with him and pulled out a photo, then passed it to Athena on his left.

"This is John and Allison Cochran and their three kids, Carter, Camille, and Clayton. They moved into this house six months ago." He took another photo from his folder and passed it to Darius on his right.

"What happened to them?" Charlie asked, pulling a small notebook and pen from her purse.

"They disappeared into thin air," Ben said. "John Cochran's sister was supposed to visit them for Christmas, and they'd started talking about the details. When she tried calling her brother with her flight information, there was no answer. According to the missing person report she filed with the police, this went on for five days. She finally called the local police, and when they did a check, they found both family cars parked in the driveway and a kitchen table set for breakfast, including two frying pans on the stove. Ready to be used."

"Did the police suspect foul play?" Athena glanced up from the photo of the house in her hand.

"The police didn't know what to make of it. There was no sign of a struggle, and they did a cursory investigation based on the reports I read." He pulled more papers from his folder and passed them around.

Will slid the photo of the family in front of Charlie and seemed to take care not to make her touch it. They exchanged glances, and she sensed unexpected empathy from him. It was as if he knew what it was like for her to hold a photo or even a report.

She carefully picked up the photo of the happy family posed outside under a tree. They all wore the same outfits. White shirts and blue jeans. The mother looked about Charlie's age, and the oldest boy looked to be about Evan's age, thirteen. The two younger children, a girl and a boy, looked to be ten and seven. All the children had their father's doe-like brown eyes and the girl had her mother's golden blonde hair. The boys looked like a miniature of their father. Charlie took a deep breath and touched the corners of the picture. Images flashed through her head of this moment. The family had gone to a local park one day last spring. The mother had wanted blooming azaleas in the picture. Wanted everything to be beautiful. Wanted everything perfect.

"John, you and Allison sit here and here," Charlie heard the photographer's voice echo through her head followed by John's and Allison's voices.

"How long is this going to take?" John grumbled. "I've got to get back to work."

"No. It's Saturday, and besides, you wanted the big house and the fancy neighborhood and all the things that go with it," Allison said through gritted teeth.

"Clayton, let's put you next to your daddy. Camille, you next to your mommy, and Carter you on the other side of your mom, okay sweetie?"

Charlie turned the photo over and found a stamp of gold ink that read Marcie Holmes Photography. Why was this day so important? Why was she seeing something that happened more than eight months ago and not something more recent? Charlie scribbled down the name before she put the photo down and slid it over to Tomeka. Will slid the missing person report in front of her. She noticed Ben studying her.

She made a face. "I didn't see anything useful. At least I don't think so. But I'd like to interview the photographer about the family."

"Sure. Just keep me informed," he said.

Charlie glanced at Tomeka next to her. She had pulled her cards out of her bag and had done a quick three-two-one spread, laying out three cards at the top, two cards touching the line of three cards and one card touching the line of two cards forming a reversed triangle. Charlie had seen her cousin Lisa use this spread before, especially for a big event in her life.

"How does it look, Tomeka?" Ben asked.

"They were in a state of normal cycles — you can see that here." She pointed to the row of three cards, her finger brushed over The Wheel of Fortune card. She sighed. "But there was this sense of being bound up. Restricted in some way," she said, touching the second card, The Hanged Man. "Then you've got Temperance here, but it's reversed, indicating a lack of long-term vision or purpose. Or it could be a sense of competition with others. Not sure which of them felt that way though. It could be the husband and he projected it onto the wife."

"Or maybe it was the wife," Charlie piped up. All eyes around the table turned to her and her cheeks burned from the sudden attention. "I just mean..." She sighed. "I saw them in the park, posing for that picture. I got the sense that she was trying to keep up with the Joneses, so to speak."

Ben nodded. "Good to know. Their neighborhood is

pretty swanky. I could see the competition between neighbors being an added pressure. What else do you see there, Tomeka?"

"It's not good, that's for sure." Tomeka pointed her long nail first at The Lovers card and then the Death card. "The Lovers card usually represents some sort of choice to be made, but it's reversed which means it was a bad choice, or a choice that someone didn't want to take responsibility for. And then there's Death." Tomeka glanced around at their faces and tapped her palm on the table. "Which doesn't mean actual death. It just means a transformation occurred." The others nodded and Charlie watched Sabine and Marigold visibly relax. "This last card is worrisome though. This is where things are headed. The Tower." Tomeka let out a shuddery breath. "This represents turmoil, death even, if the situation is right. Grief, anger, terror. Danger." Her dark red-tipped fingernail touched the single card at the bottom of the triangle of cards. "Darkness."

"So they're alive?" Ben asked.

Tomeka's chest rose and fell with a deep sigh. "That's not really clear. Possibly. If they are alive, they won't be for long."

Ben clenched his jaw, and his eyes darkened with the intensity of his gaze. "That just means we have to act fast. Athena, I need you and Sabine to look into any similar cases that may have occurred in the last year. If you find nothing, go out five years."

Athena jotted down his instructions on a yellow legal pad.

"We should also look at the victims. Who they were. If they had any enemies. Or any big changes in their lives," Charlie blurted out. She slapped her hand over her mouth. "I'm sorry. I didn't mean to—"

"No, that's great, Charlie. Your instincts are right," Ben said.

"It's not really my instincts as much as it is working cases with Jason. If Athena and Sabine find other victims, then we can look at their commonalities," Charlie said. "Which could give us insight into whoever took them."

"How do we know it's not just ordinary kidnappers?" Will asked. "Why is the DOL involved?"

"That's a good question and a simple one to answer. They're witches."

"You just said they were having Christmas," Sabine said.

"Yes. It's easy to pass off Yule as Christmas, especially if their extended family were not practicing witches," Ben explained.

"True," Athena said. "My mother still puts up a nativity scene for my grandmother's sake."

There were several nods around the table, and Charlie shifted in her chair. Jen always did the planning and decorating for all the holidays. With the beginning of Yule coming up next week, a pang of guilt filled her. She'd been ignoring Jen's requests to help decorate this year. Making excuses about being too busy with the job change over.

"I did cursory scouting of the location and found these." Ben took two more photos from his folder and passed them around. The images looked almost like a negative. Symbols drawn on the front door of the house, and on every window – sigils. Charlie had seen them used in witchcraft before.

"So, you think a witch did this?" Charlie studied one of the photos.

"Possibly," Ben said.

"Why?" Charlie asked.

"As soon as we find him or her, I intend to ask. If not a witch, then possibly a demon, or even a ghost," Ben said. "Marigold, I want you and Tomeka to work together on building out our case. We'll use this room as our home base for now. So, tape up pictures and document everything we find."

"You got it, sir," Marigold said. "If you bring me back some personal effects of the family, I'll start scrying."

"I don't know how to do that," Tomeka said, sinking down in her seat a little.

"No worries," Marigold chirped. "You use cards, right?"

Tomeka nodded. "It's just another form of prognostication. I'm betting you'll pick it up easily."

"Okay," Tomeka said in a breathy voice.

Darius nudged his sister with his elbow. She painted a smile on her face and nodded.

"Great," Tomeka said. "You don't use a crystal ball, do you?"

"No. I use water," Marigold said. "And I'll take precautions to ensure my safety, and yours, too."

"Charlie and Will, that leaves you with me," Ben said.

Charlie exchanged a glance with Will and gave him a perfunctory smile.

"Everybody clear on their assignments?"

A murmur of yeses went around the room.

"Let's get to it then. The clock is ticking."

CHARLIE AND WILL FOLLOWED BEN TO THE FOURTH FLOOR to an open space filled with identical workspaces. Each worktable reminded Charlie of a small kitchen island with a butcher block top and a tall, well-padded stool centered between two cabinet bases. On top of the surface sat a mortar and pestle, an electronic tablet with a cover that turned into a stand, and a Bluetooth keyboard.

"Very high tech," Will said. He picked up the tablet at

the workstation with a nameplate that read William J. Tucker.

"That's mainly for reports, expenses, and any digital research we need to do on the road," Ben said.

"I've got a laptop I use for my vamp stuff," Will said.

"You mean your hacking?" Ben said with a wry expression.

"Maybe," Will smirked. "Maybe it just holds all my porn."

The two men laughed, and Charlie tried to ignore them. She didn't want to know if Ben also had a computer with porn on it.

"Charlie, you okay with a tablet?" Ben asked.

"Sure," Charlie said. "I'm okay with computer stuff, I guess."

"Good," Will said. "I know some witches are more likely to fry something electronic."

"My aunt Evangeline does. It's why she doesn't like smartphones."

"I don't blame her," Ben said.

"So where do you want to start, boss?" Will tucked the tablet into the leather bag he had slung across his body. Charlie spotted the hilt of a large knife before he closed the flap and fastened the buckle.

"I want us to head over to the house," Ben said. "Take a look around. See what we find."

"Have the cops already been there?" Will asked.

"They have, but they're not looking for the same things we are. "

"Right," Will said dryly. "All the witchy things."

Charlie suppressed a snicker and grabbed her bag. "We've got a two-hour drive, and I want to talk to that photographer today, too, if possible."

"We better get a move on then," Ben said.

CHAPTER 3

The house on Mulberry Lane looked perfect from the outside. Tall, straight lines of brick Georgian façade, the manicured yard complete with thick borders of pansies, and hedges of carved balls of boxwood suggested wealth. But it was a wealthy neighborhood full of similar houses on wooded one-acre lots. More than anything, Charlie sensed anxiety in this neighborhood. It pervaded everything. What did rich people have to be so anxious about? But she already knew the answer to that question, didn't she? Scott, her ex-husband, came from wealth, and she sometimes sensed the same anxiety from his family, from his neighbors. Everybody wanting to impress everybody else. She'd felt it when they were married, and she felt it now from every single house they passed. Her life might be simpler now, and she still had to count her pennies, even with this new job and increased pay, but she wouldn't trade any of it for that constant, low-level thrum of anxiety that permeated her life before she'd left Scott.

Ben drove up the circular driveway and parked in front. The yellow police tape across the double black front doors had come loose and now flapped in the slight breeze. The three of them hopped out of Ben's restored FJ50, and Ben opened the front door with a simple unlocking spell after he sliced through the secondary tape the police had installed between the double front doors.

The smell of brimstone stung Charlie's nostrils when she entered the foyer. A sparkly yellow dust hung in the air.

"Oh, hell," Ben muttered.

"Demons," Will said pushing past Charlie and Ben. He reached into his bag and pulled out a small flask with a cross on it.

Charlie caught up to him. She held her wand in her hand, gripping the hilt of the carved wood tightly. "Holy water?"

"Yep," he said. He walked into the living room and glanced around. Something in the fireplace seemed to catch his attention, and he approached it with caution. He knelt on the carpet next to the stone hearth. A black smudge darkened the brick lining of the firebox, which was strange because there were gas logs. The family had never burned wood in the fireplace that Charlie could tell.

"What do you think that is?" Charlie asked.

Will reached inside his bag and took out a small glass vial and a buck knife. He unfolded the blade and scraped the sooty layer, leaving a clean line through it. He brought the knife to his nose and sniffed it before he carefully scraped it into the vial.

"What are you going to do with that?" Charlie asked, intrigued by his methods.

"He's going to test it for different residues," Ben said.

"It could be paper," Will said, corking the top of the vial and tucking it back into his bag. He closed the blade of the knife and slipped it into his front pocket. "But it could be something a little more hellish, too."

"How very forensic of you," Charlie quipped.

"Girl, I got *skillz*," Will said with a glint in his eyes.

Charlie laughed. "Goddess help us all."

"Are you sensing anything, Charlie?" Ben asked.

She glanced around and found more of the family photos like the ones Ben had shown them in the conference room. She picked up one of the frames and touched the faces of the family. The voices of a man and woman echoed through her head.

"You're kidding me, right," he said, his voice full of

derision and disgust. "You can't seriously be thinking about paying five hundred dollars for photos."

"We can't live in this house and not have family photos like everyone else. Margot Baxter already noticed that we didn't have any," she countered. "You're the one who wanted to be here. We have to do what everyone else does. Otherwise, Carter, Clayton, and Camille will never fit in. We're doing this for them, remember?"

Money — it could make things better when you had it or way, way worse when you didn't. Bunny, Charlie's grandmother, always said that money was a mindset. "If you want, want, want, then you'll be blessed (or cursed in Charlie's opinion) with lack, lack, lack because nothing's ever enough to fill up that hole. If you thank, thank, thank the goddess, you'll be blessed with more of what you're thankful for, Charlie girl."

"They were struggling financially," Charlie said. She put the photo back on the mantle.

"I can't imagine why," Ben said, his voice full of sarcasm.

The living room was full of expensive-looking furniture. Some antique, some more contemporary. Charlie ran her hand over a leather wingback chair near the fireplace, and the supple, buttery skin yielded to her touch.

"Jason always says that crimes are usually about two things — money or love," Charlie said. "We should check their financials, see where they're getting their money from. What did you say they did for a living?"

"He had a successful insurance agency, I believe," Ben chimed in. "I'll see what Athena and Marigold can dig up on the money front."

"Sounds like this Jason is a wise man," Will said. "Although doing what I do, I'd add hunger to that list, especially when it comes to vamps and werewolves."

An image of a werewolf's snarling bloody snout popped into Charlie's head and she shivered.

"Can't argue with that," Charlie said. "I'd probably add demons and even certain spirits to that hunger list."

Will met her eyes and gave her a nod, and she saw the look. A spark of attraction. Charlie glanced away toward the bookshelves. She couldn't deny that she found him attractive too. But she loved Tom and there was something about Will, something she couldn't quite put her finger on that made her a little nervous. She was going to have to let him know she had a boyfriend, but in a subtle way. The last thing she wanted was for things to be awkward with her new teammate.

"You're smarter than I thought you'd be," Will said.

"Oh-kay," Charlie said. "Thank you?"

"That's my fault," Ben said.

Charlie gave Ben a quizzical look. "I told him you were very intuitive. I should've added smart, too."

"Yeah, you should have," Will said. "I'm gonna head

31

upstairs to check it out. Charlie, you want to check the kitchen and whatever else is down here?"

"Sure," she said.

"There's a basement in this place, so I'm going to have a look," Ben said. "Give a shout if you need help."

"Of course," Charlie said and turned to the closed French doors of the dining room.

"Hey, Charlie," Ben said. "Don't be afraid to use your wand. There could be hidden threats here."

"Okay." Charlie gave him a reassuring smile and watched him go through a door beneath the stairs.

Her belly tightened into a knot. Pulling out her wand had always meant either she was about to perform a ritual, or she needed to defend herself. She'd never just used it to use it, but she supposed now, just like Jason pulled his gun in certain situations to clear a space, she had to do the same thing. She sighed and reluctantly pointed her wand, hoping she'd never have to use it.

CHARLIE SLIPPED INTO THE DINING ROOM, HER WAND gripped tightly in one hand. The curtains were drawn closed and probably made of a dense, heavy fabric because only a thin strip of light showed around the edges and top. She flipped the light switch, and the compact fluorescent bulbs flickered to life, buzzed loudly, then went dark. The acrid scent of electrical ions and smoke stung Charlie's nose. She flipped the light switch off.

"So that's how you're going to be," she said aloud to no one in particular. She reached into her bag and fished out a small flashlight that Jason had given her. She held her wand tip down and shined the light into all the corners of the dining room. The yellow-tinged gold dust floated in the beam, and the spoiled-egg aroma of sulfur hung in the air.

A demon had definitely passed through here. But why? On paper, this family seemed so ordinary compared to the witches she knew— even though Charlie had sensed the wife just wanted them to look perfect, to fit in, which was an expensive proposition in this neighborhood.

When she cleared the room, she stepped into the kitchen, and immediately the stench of rotting meat slapped her in the face and the sound of flies buzzing around her head made her duck. She shined the light over every surface of the kitchen. Her stomach lurched, and she covered her mouth, retching and gagging at the sight of so much blood. Charlie turned away quickly and bolted out of the kitchen, back through the dining room and living room to the foyer.

"Ben!"

Charlie threw the front door open, not stopping until

she reached the bottom of the porch steps. She gulped the fresh sweet air and bent over with her hands on her knees to keep the dizziness from spinning through her head.

"Charlie?" Ben touched her back. "What happened? Are you okay?"

"There's so much blood," Charlie said. She spit, trying to get the taste of rot and coppery blood out of her mouth. "Why didn't the cops mention the blood?"

"What are you talking about?" Ben said.

Charlie wiped her mouth with the back of her hand and stood up straight. She looked him in the eye.

"In the kitchen. The island, the counters, even the walls are covered with blood."

"Charlie, there was no report of blood in any of the police reports."

"What? That doesn't make any sense."

"I don't know what else to tell you."

"That kitchen is covered in blood," Charlie insisted and folded her arms.

"I believe you," Ben said. "I'm just confounded, I guess. Will you go back in with me? We can check it out together."

Charlie grimaced, but said, "Of course."

A few moments later, having recovered slightly, Charlie took a deep breath and followed Ben into the kitchen. She braced herself for the sickening sight.

"Okay, show me where you saw the blood." Ben stepped back and let her pass him.

The faint scent of bleach infused the air. The white subway tiles shined against the Carrera marble countertops and the pale gray cabinets looked freshly painted. The long island in the center of the kitchen had a decorative basket with boxwood greenery and gold and silver balls. Someone had been preparing for Yule. Charlie turned in a circle and shook her head. There was no yellow dust floating about like the other rooms they'd encountered. Every surface gleamed as if they'd been freshly scrubbed. The round table in the adjacent nook was set with three place settings and empty juice glasses.

Charlie's heart sank to her stomach like a cold rock. "What the hell? It was here. I swear there was blood. And the air stank — like rotting meat. I even heard flies buzzing."

"I believe you, Charlie," Ben said.

"You do?"

"Of course, why wouldn't I?"

"I—I guess I'm just used to having to argue my point," she said. "Sorry."

"No worries, all right? I've got your back, and I'm totally relying on you to see things I can't."

A soft smile crept across her lips and she nodded. "Thanks. I appreciate that."

Ben gave her a nod and then turned back to view the kitchen. "So, there was blood."

"A lot of blood. And from the stench, some sort of meat. I don't even want to imagine what that could mean," Charlie said.

"Right. The question is, whose blood? And who cleaned it up?"

"Yeah," Charlie said. "There's no demon dust in here."

"Whoever cleaned up, must've vacuumed it all up when they were scrubbing this place down."

"Maybe," Charlie said.

"You have a different thought?" Ben asked.

"I'm not sure what I think at this point. It's just weird, that's all."

"Agreed," Ben said.

"Did you find anything in the basement?"

"Not really," he said.

"Where do you want to go next?" Charlie asked.

"Let's go upstairs. Check the bedrooms. Maybe you'll get some impressions there."

Charlie pursed her lips and nodded. "Fine."

CHARLIE FOUND WILL IN THE MASTER BEDROOM CLOSET searching the pockets of John Cochran's suit jackets.

"What are you looking for?" Charlie asked.

Will turned and smiled. "People stick stuff in their pockets all the time. Dry cleaning tickets. Receipts. Change. It could lead us to a clue or two. I always like to check a person's pockets, just to see what sort of story it will tell me."

Charlie chuckled. "What's the weirdest thing you've ever found in someone's pockets?"

"I was on the trail of a vamp nest about a year ago. One of the victims used to collect the fortunes out of fortune cookies. He had a jar of them, and he'd take them and arrange them on index cards into poetry. I found several index cards in one of his pockets."

"Poetry from fortune cookies? Wow. That never would've even crossed my mind."

"It was actually kinda interesting, if you like poetry that is," Will said.

"So I take it you haven't found any poetry in these pockets," Charlie asked.

"'Fraid not." He lifted a small key attached to an orange fob. "I did, however, find this."

"What is it?" she asked.

"It's a key to a locker in a bus station."

"Does it say which station?" She took the key and inspected it.

"Yep. I'm thinking we know our next stop," Will said.

"Great," Charlie said. She handed the key back to him and turned away from the closet. "Let me finish checking out the rest of this floor and then we'll go tell Ben."

"Deal," he said and pocketed the key. "I'll see if anything else turns up in here."

Charlie left Will to finish searching the closet and decided to take on the bathroom. She'd seen mirrors used as portals before. If a demon had passed through from his realm to this one, without an invitation, then a mirror seemed like the easiest point of entry.

Charlie flipped on the light in the master bath. A range of gray glass subway tiles lined the walls of the steam shower and walls behind the modern standalone soaking tub. The white quartz counters had flecks of silver. Square, shallow sink bowls sat on top of the counter in front of a long mirror in a black bamboo frame. Charlie inspected the mirror for signs of spirit travel, such as the silver metal on the back fading or ghostly handprints, but nothing revealed itself to her, and her senses didn't pick up anything otherworldly. She glanced around the room again and noticed it, like the kitchen, didn't have a speck of the yellow-gold dust. . No demon had wandered in here. She flipped off the light and moved on to inspect the other bedrooms.

In the hall leading to the kid's bedrooms, a wall of photos stared out over the space. Charlie stopped a moment to look at the perfectly-timed candid shots mixed with professional studio photos. Three faded rectangles on the wall pointed to three missing frames. Charlie touched the wall where they'd been, trying to get a sense of what might have happened. An image of John Cochran flashed in her head. He was struggling to open the back of one of the frames. An overwhelming feeling of desperation spread through her fingers, up her arm, and into her torso. Frantic thoughts — his thoughts — raced through her head.

Have to get them for him. Have to call him. Have to create an offering. Have to...have to...have to.

The glass to the frame broke in his hand, slicing his palm, slicing through his thoughts. He dropped the frame and sucked on his bloody thumb. The coppery taste on his tongue made his stomach groan.

Charlie jerked her hand away and took a step back. Something crunched beneath her foot, and she lifted her shoe. She shined her light down, and small glass shards glittered. Whoever had cleaned up the broken frame must have missed it. She knelt to pick it up and found a speck of dried blood. Gently, she touched her thumb to the drop of blood and closed her eyes.

"Daddy? What are you doing?"

"Nothing, Camille. Go on, get out of here. Go play downstairs."

"That's my baby picture," Camille said. "What are you doing with it? Mama said it's our keepsake."

A growl started low in his throat, and he turned on the girl. "I said go play downstairs."

The child whimpered and slunk away, being careful to stay out of his reach. She hated him when he was like this. Her tender little foot seared with pain, and she cried out. Camille fell to the floor, her long blonde hair covering her eyes. She bent her knee so she could look at the bottom of her foot. A small shard of broken glass had pierced her heel.

"Daddy?" Camille looked up at him, but he'd returned to taking the other keepsake frames off the wall. The ones for Carter and Clayton.

"Daddy, I'm bleeding." He just ignored her. Camille sniffed and gently plucked the glass from her foot and dropped it on the carpet, then limped away calling for her mother.

Charlie reached into her pocket and pulled out a small plastic bag. With a sharpie, she'd written Evidence on it. She slipped the piece of glass inside, folded it up, and put it in her pocket. She didn't know what it meant or why John Cochran would need the baby photos from the missing frames, but maybe with a little help, she would figure it out.

"ANYTHING UPSTAIRS?" BEN ASKED WHEN CHARLIE rejoined him in the living room.

"Maybe," she said. "Did Will show you the key?"

"Yeah. We can head over there now, unless you have something else you want us to look at here."

Charlie pulled the bag with the glass from her pocket. "I found this on the floor. I had...uh...a vision."

"Okay. What'd you see?" Ben asked.

"I saw the father frantically pulling frames off the walls. He broke the glass from one of them." She held up the glass as proof and tapped the spot of blood. "This is the girl's. She stepped on it while he was pulling the frames apart. He didn't even look at her when she cried out in pain."

"And that's important?" Ben asked.

"Oh yeah. He's her father. I don't know of any parent that would ignore their crying child. I mean, how they react to the crying could run the gamut from compassionate to violent, but he didn't even flinch. It was like he was –"

"Possessed?" Ben asked.

"Maybe. It's hard to say though. His thoughts kept running through my head. He needed the pictures. For him," she said.

"Him who?" Ben asked.

Charlie shrugged. "Your guess is as good as mine. Do

you have a picture of the family I can take home with me?"

"Um..." Ben looked around and a moment later picked up a framed photo of the family from the mantel. "Take this one."

"You sure?"

"Yep," he said.

"Didn't you say the family reported them missing? Do you think they'll miss this?"

"Yeah. The husband's sister did," Ben said. "I'm sure she won't mind since we're looking for the family at her request. I couldn't find any family on the wife's side."

"That's really sad. And a little strange, isn't it?"

Ben gave her a thoughtful look. "I don't have any family, so it doesn't seem that strange to me."

"Ben. You have family. You have--" Charlie began.

"Hey, boss," Will poked his head into the living room from the foyer. "Nosy neighbor alert."

"Okay, thanks," Ben said. "We should get out of here."

"I thought that the DOL worked with local and federal police," Charlie said.

"They do," Ben said. "But discretion is always the name of the game."

"Right," Charlie said.

The doorbell rang.

"I'll handle her. Why don't you and Will slip out the back door and make your way around to the car."

"No problem, boss," Will said.

"Fine," Charlie said.

Charlie led Will to the kitchen and stopped short when she reached the door. The smell of blood smacked her in the face again. She covered her nose and mouth with her hand out of instinct more than anything else.

"What's wrong?" Will asked.

"Nothing." Charlie lowered her hand and braced herself to enter the kitchen again. She squeezed the grip of her wand, held her breath and stepped through the door, expecting to see blood everywhere.

Instead, she saw a little girl standing behind the island. The same little girl she'd seen in her vision earlier. The child's eyes widened at the sight of them, and she hunkered down behind the island.

"Camille?" Charlie said.

"Who's Camille?" Will asked.

Charlie pressed a finger to her lips and, as quietly as she could, slipped between the counter and the island toward the girl.

"It's okay, honey," Charlie said. "I'm here to help you."

Charlie peeked around the corner of the island but found no one there. Her heart sank. That meant only one thing. Camille Cochran was dead. Something pale yellow caught her eye and she moved to where she could see better. At the base of the cabinet was a battered yellow and white teddy bear. Charlie picked it up, brown splotches splattered across the bear's legs matted the faux fur.

"What is that?" Will asked. He stood too close to her. She could feel his hot breath on her neck.

"Could you please take a step back?"

"Sure." He held up his hands in surrender and did as she asked. "Sorry."

"No, it's me. I just have this thing about personal space."

"Because of your..." he twirled his fingers, as if it might help him complete the sentence.

"My what?" Charlie asked.

"Your psychic thing."

"Ability. Yeah, something like that," she said, not masking her irritation. "Let's just get out of here. Okay?"

"Fine," Will said. He stepped back to let her pass. "Ladies first."

Charlie held onto the bear, wishing she'd brought a larger bag for evidence. She pushed past Will toward the back door.

The cool, crisp, fresh air wrapped around her, and she stepped out on the back deck to breathe it in.

"Come on," Will said. He made his way down the steps to the back yard. "We should hurry up."

Charlie scowled and followed him to the side yard. The two of them slipped through the gate and made their way to the car on the street. Charlie saw Ben on the front porch talking to the neighbor. Maybe even asking her questions about the Cochrans. His gaze shifted from the neighbor to her and Will. Charlie gave him a little wave before getting into the passenger side of his truck. A couple of minutes later, Ben and the neighbor walked down the steps together.

Ben got into the driver's seat. He waved and smiled as the cute soccer mom in her yoga pants and expensive athletic shoes flashed a smile his way.

Charlie gave Ben a disapproving look.

"What did she say?" Charlie asked.

"Oh, you know, just how concerned she was about the disappearance of her neighbors. How they were nice people. How her daughter was best friends with their daughter. How scared she was for the neighborhood," Ben said. "The usual BS."

"You think she was lying?" Charlie asked.

"I think she's just like them, full of secrets."

"Aren't we all," Will muttered and settled into a relaxed position in the back seat.

CHAPTER 4

C harlie drove down the long driveway to her little house, glad to be home. She probably should've gotten a hotel room like Ben had, but she didn't sleep well in strange places, especially places where unknown people slept, where they left little pieces of themselves for her to stumble over like a rock on a path. It was only a two-hour drive to Columbia tomorrow, to the bus station matching the key Will had found.

It surprised her to see the lights on, glowing warm and cozy through the shears covering her windows, but it also warmed her heart. Tom was waiting for her inside. They'd exchanged keys just after Thanksgiving. It had been her idea and it had started out under the guise of Tom feeding her kitten, Poe, if she couldn't make it home from Charlotte in time. But that had been a lie, hadn't it? Yes. She just wanted him to be able to come and go as he pleased under the formality of her permission. He had given her a key to the mortuary, which still seemed odd to her but she understood his desire to reciprocate. As a reaper, he had no need for a house or an apartment. He spent most of his days and nights, when not with her, tending to the dead in one way or another.

As she approached the house, she could feel his energy buzzing around, a strange and glorious feeling. She pulled into her parking spot next to his black Ford Fusion and hopped out. Her feet barely touched the ground as she hurried across the gravel drive, and up the steps into her house.

The scent of herb-roasted chicken filled her senses and her mouth watered. A mewling black ball of fur rushed at her and she scooped Poe up in her arms.

"Well hello there," she whispered against Poe's ears. "Did you miss me? I sure missed you." She planted a kiss on top of Poe's head and held her close. "Tom? Are you here?"

He popped his head around the short wall dividing the kitchen from the living room. "You're home." He wiped his hands on a dishtowel and threw it over his shoulder. "Dinner's almost ready."

"Oh my goddess, it smells so good. Much better than the fast-food burger I stopped and got for dinner." She crossed the living room in a few steps and planted a kiss squarely on his lips. He deftly removed the kitten from her place beneath Charlie's chin and shifted the purring black fluff into his arms.

"Oh no, I should've texted you about dinner," Tom said. "I didn't even think you might stop and get something on the way home."

"I didn't. I mean, I did, but I haven't eaten it. And whatever you're cooking will be divine in comparison."

"Divine, huh?" he said.

"Yes, sir." She leaned in and kissed him again.

"Perhaps you should go check out the bathroom." Tom spoke against her lips while he stroked the kitten's fur.

Charlie pulled back a little and studied his face. "The bathroom? Why?"

"You'll see. Go on," Tom said.

Charlie reluctantly made her way to the small bathroom adjacent to her bedroom and the living room.

When she flipped on the light, it became apparent why Tom had wanted her to take a look. A whole roll of toilet paper had been pulled off the roll and shredded into a million tiny pieces. Charlie gasped and turned to eye the purring offender in Tom's arms.

"Oh my goodness, Poe. What did you do? Did you shred all that paper?" She retrieved the kitten from Tom and looked her in the eyes. "Did you do this?"

"Are you expecting an answer?" Tom asked.

Charlie chuckled and scratched the kitten behind the ears before kissing her again and gently placing her on the floor.

"Don't worry. I'll clean it up," she said.

"I don't care about the toilet paper. I figured you'd get a kick out of it." He brushed his hand along her cheek and kissed her. Charlie leaned into him and he wrapped his arms around her waist and drew her close, deepening the kiss. She pulled away and sighed, then nestled against his neck, breathing him in.

He kissed her temple and held her tight.

"Should I ask how your day was? Or is this affection an indication?"

"The DOL's fine." She shrugged. "So far, anyway. I'm not sure I like my new partner. He's a bit... gruff."

"More so than Jason?" Tom said, sounding astonished.

"Oh yeah. This guy's a vampire hunter. And he has seen some darkness."

"I could say the same of you, and you're not gruff," Tom said.

"I know. He's just a puzzle that I guess I'll have to figure out," she said. "Hot one minute, cold the next."

"Well, why don't we have some dinner, and then you can take a nice hot bubble bath."

"That sounds great," Charlie said. She lifted her face

and kissed him on his neck near the base of his ear and whispered, "Maybe you can join me."

"As you wish, my love," Tom hugged her tighter. "As you wish."

* * *

THE NEXT MORNING, BEFORE CHARLIE HEADED OUT OF town, she stopped at The Kitchen Witch Café to say hello to her cousin and to grab some breakfast. She often ate at her cousin's restaurant, but this was the first time that she could ever remember being at the restaurant only minutes after it opened.

"Good morning," Jen Holloway chirped from behind the counter. "I was hoping you'd stop by. I want to hear everything about your first day."

"And I would love to tell you everything, but unfortunately I have to get my breakfast to go. And maybe my lunch, if possible," Charlie said. "I don't think I can do fast food two days in a row."

"Can't blame you there," Jen said. "I'll see what I can whip up. Would you mind taking extra to Ben?"

"Of course not," Charlie said.

"Great." Jen perched a pen to her order pad. "What can I get you for breakfast?"

"I will take a pork chop biscuit and a large iced tea," Charlie said.

Jen scribbled the order on the ticket. "Coming right up."

Jen put the ticket on the order wheel and gave it a spin. She filled a glass with ice, poured fresh iced tea over it, then placed it in front of Charlie. "While you wait."

"Thanks," Charlie said, taking a sip.

"So, are you heading back to Charlotte today?" Jen asked.

"I'm meeting Ben and Will in Columbia first, and then we'll head to Charlotte."

"Why don't you just get a hotel like Ben does?" Jen asked. "All this driving is hard on the body."

"Well, mainly because no matter how clean you think a hotel room is, it isn't. At least not for me. I pick up too much of what people leave behind. If you know what I mean."

Jen scrunched her elfin face, and her nose wrinkled with disgust. "Ew."

"Ew is right," Charlie said. "Anyway, it's not that bad of a commute. And it's only every other week."

"True," Jen said. "So, we're decorating the tree Friday night and I'd like to talk about plans for the day Yule starts. I'm thinking about another bonfire. Everyone seems to enjoy them so much."

"A bonfire sounds good. I'm not much of a decorator though."

"But you're coming for the solstice, right? It's the start of Yule," Jen said.

"I don't know." Charlie shrugged. "I need to check to see which holidays I get off."

Jen made an indignant sound. Charlie's phone chirped, letting her know she had a new text. She pulled her phone from the front pocket of her purse.

"Sorry, it's Evan." Charlie held up one finger. Jen scowled and picked up a clean rag and began to wipe down the counter a little too fervently for Charlie's liking. She focused on the screen in her hand and began to read.

Hey Mom — how do I cast a spell to help my basketball team win their game this week?

You don't.

Mom. Come on. Please?

No. Absolutely not. You're not to be practicing witchcraft on your own. There can be dire consequences if you do. Don't you remember Thanksgiving?

Of course I do. Dad's still moping around.

I know. And he will for a while.

So there's no spell to help him?

No honey. Only time can heal that wound.

So how about the winning spell for my team? That one exists, right?

We will talk about it this weekend.

It'll be too late by then. My game is Friday.

If you really want to win, you'd better practice.

Fine.

A smiling poop emoji appeared on her screen. Charlie frowned.

"What's the matter?" Jen asked.

"Does this mean what I think it means?" Charlie showed Jen the phone. An amused expression lined her cousin's elfin features.

"It just means he's disappointed. If he were older I would think something else, but since it's Evan, I'm pretty sure it's just his disappointment," Jen said.

"Oh," Charlie said. She put the phone down on the counter. "Well, unfortunately, disappointment's part of life. Something he has to get used to."

"I see he's excited about exploring his abilities," Jen said.

"Yes," Charlie said. "You could say that. Although I have given him specific instructions that he is not to do any sort of witchcraft or magic without supervision."

"That can be tough when you're his age. I remember all too well trying to spread my wings once I came into my gifts. You should talk to Evangeline about how she handled it. She did a good job with Lisa and me, and Daphne, of course."

"That's a good idea," Charlie said. "The last thing I need is for him to go off on his own without proper instruction. It could be dangerous."

"I totally agree," Jen said. "Thankfully, I don't have to worry about that for a few more years with Ruby."

"Teaching Ruby will be a piece of cake," Charlie said. "You don't have to deal with her dad about what's right or appropriate."

"Thank goodness for that," Jen said. "Now about the solstice--"

"Order up." Charlie heard Manny the cook's voice, but she couldn't see him behind the pass-through window.

Jen held up one finger. "Just a second. I'm not done discussing this." She grabbed three bags from the window, slipped utensils and extra napkins inside the bigger bag, and folded down the tops. "I had him make two lunches, so if you wouldn't mind giving one to Ben."

"Of course not," Charlie glanced at her watch. "I'm sorry to do this, hon, but I've got to get going."

"So, do you think you'll be home tonight?" Jen asked.

"That is the plan," Charlie said.

"Great, we can talk about the solstice then. You and Tom are invited for dinner and I want to hear all about your new job."

"You don't want to wait until Friday night dinner?" Charlie asked.

"No, that's too far away. I want all the details, plus we'll be so busy decorating." Jen grinned.

"Sure, decorating." Charlie gave her cousin a half-hearted smile. "What about Ben?"

"Oh, well he's invited too if he wants to drive all the way back. But he won't. He'll stay in Charlotte. And I can talk to him anytime about his job. Or at least as much as he'll tell me. And he has no interest in decorating a tree for solstice. I'm hoping a bonfire will entice him to at least come for the first night of Yule."

"Okay. Sounds good," Charlie said. "I'll text Tom and let him know about dinner. Thanks."

CHAPTER 5

Charlie arrived at the bus station by 8:30 AM. She didn't see Ben's car yet so she took a moment to look through the bag Jen had prepared for them. She found two fruit cups, some fresh coleslaw, and two pimento cheese sandwiches that were generous on the cheese spread and light on the bread. Just the way Charlie liked it. She would pick up some potato chips when she stopped to fill up with gas.

A knock on the window startled her, and she jumped a little. Ben and Will stood outside the door of her Honda. Will nodded and Ben waved. She quickly folded up the paper bag and shoved it into her messenger bag for safekeeping. She hadn't thought to get something for Will. He would have to be on his own for lunch. She got out of the car and locked the door behind her.

"Good morning, boys," she said.

"Sorry we're late," Ben said.

Charlie glanced at the watch on her wrist. "It looks like you're right on time to me. So, are y'all ready to check out this locker?"

"Yes, ma'am." Will jingled the key in his hand.

"Did you have any dreams last night?" Ben asked.

"I did not. Or at least not anything about this case. Am I expected to dream as part of my job?" Charlie asked.

"No," Ben chuckled. "I just know that sometimes you do. I thought maybe we might get a little lucky."

"Sorry," Charlie said. "But that doesn't mean I won't dream tonight. By the way, Jen says hey. She sent breakfast and lunch for you." She handed him the bag.

A pleased smile spread across Ben's face. The bag crinkled when he unrolled the top and peered inside. "Anything good?"

"It's from Jen. Of course, it's good. She sent pimento cheese sandwiches for lunch. Not sure what she sent you for breakfast. Will, I'm sorry I didn't think to get you one."

"No problem," Will said. "I'm more partial to hamburgers than other kind of sandwiches."

"Good to know," Charlie said.

"Are y'all ready to get this party started?" Will asked.

"Lead the way." Charlie gestured to the building.

A few minutes later, they huddled in front of a row

of tall lockers ranging in size from small square cubbies to long, full-sized lockers. It didn't take long for Will to comb through the numbers and find the door matching the key. Charlie held her breath when he slipped the key into the lock, turned it, and carefully opened the door.

Charlie noticed Ben rubbing his thumb across the fingertips of his right hand. He stood ready to call up whatever magic might be needed should they find something they had to contain, or worse, kill.

Her heartbeat thrummed in her ears. She let out a quiet breath once Will opened the door.

"What the hell?" Will said. He reached for the leather-bound book, but Ben grabbed his arm, pulling him away.

"Don't touch that," Ben said.

"Why not?" Will asked.

Charlie leaned in and inspected the thick book. On the front cover a tree with curled branches had been carved into the leather and on the spine strange writing was etched into the leather. Charlie's heartbeat sped up as soon as she realized what it was.

"I think it's cursed," Charlie said.

"What do you mean?" Will said.

"What she means," Ben said darkly, "is that there's a possible curse on the spine of that book. Whoever touches it, except for its master, will die an excruciating horrible death. Possibly. We won't know for sure until we get it back to the office and run some tests on it."

"Jesus," Will said, under his breath. "Do I want to know what excruciating, horrible death means?"

"It probably would be different for all of us. We're not the master of the book, so it might be that the curse is very individualized. My horrible death would not be the same as yours," Charlie said.

"Lovely," Will said, clearly not amused. "Sounds more like a witch thing than a demon thing. Figures."

Charlie bristled. Why was he working with witches if he didn't like them? She thought about asking him but stopped herself. The last thing she needed was to upset Ben since he was her boss now.

"Who do you think hid it here?" Charlie asked. "Husband or wife?"

"My money's on the husband," Will said. "I found the key in his pocket."

"Maybe but if I was the wife trying to hide something from my possibly possessed husband, I might hide the key to its location in his pocket," Charlie said. "Especially if I were devious enough to put a curse on a book and I wanted him to find it."

"That's a scary way of looking at it. So you think the wife hid the key hoping her husband would find this book and it would what? Curse him dead?" Will asked.

"Maybe." Charlie folded her arms across her chest. "I

don't have a good sense of her yet. And we don't know if it's a book or who it belongs to. It could be the thing that helped him summon the demon."

"Charlie's right, it could be either one of them. We won't know until we open the book."

"And exactly how are we going to do that?" Will asked.

"We're going to have to extract it carefully. I'll call in some reinforcements. We need a special container." He pulled his phone from his pocket, quickly thumbed through his contacts, and made a call.

"Hey, Lauren. It's Ben," he began and walked away out of earshot.

"So are you?" Will asked.

"Am I what?" Charlie asked.

"Devious?" A sly smile spread across his lips.

"Only if I have to be," she said. "What about you?"

"Same," he said. "Looks like we finally have something in common."

"Sure," Charlie said, rolling her eyes.

"You don't like me," he said.

"I like you fine," she said. "You're just different than my old partner. I'm sorry if I seem a little distant, I guess."

"Right," he said. "Ben said that you were working for the police before."

"I was. I still am. When time allows."

"Sure," Will said. "What do you do for them?"

"Mainly I help with cold cases and missing people. Every once in a while, a murder," she said, downplaying her role.

"Oh, I see. How long have you been a witch?" he asked.

"Well, I was born a witch. Although I didn't start seriously practicing until almost two years ago. It's in my family."

"So, you're what they call a natural-born witch then?" he asked.

"Something like that, yeah," she said. "How about you? How did you become a vampire hunter?"

"When I was a kid, my best friend was turned into a vampire. My friends and I hunted down his maker and killed her. That's how I got the scar." He pointed to the long scraggly white line running along his jaw.

"I'm so sorry. That's terrible. How old were you?"

"Thirteen."

Charlie's stomach churned. Evan was thirteen. She could not even conceive of her little boy hunting down a vampire and killing it. A thirteen-year-old was just a child.

"You look surprised," he said.

"My son is thirteen. I can't even fathom him having the maturity to go on a vampire hunt. What happened to your friend? The one that was turned?"

"Okay, so here's what's going happen," Ben said,

approaching them again. "Lauren's going to send some backup, and we're gonna take that book out, put it in a lead box, and take it back to the headquarters. We'll examine it in one of the clean rooms."

Ben's gaze shifted from Charlie to Will and back to Charlie. "Everything okay?"

"Everything's just dandy, boss," Will said. "I saw a diner down the street. Since y'all have your lunch, I'm gonna head down there and get a late breakfast before the backup gets here."

"Sure. I'll join you," Ben said. "I'll save the sandwich for a snack or something later. It may just end up being dinner. Charlie, you want to join us?"

"Sure," she said. "I'm not very hungry, but I can have a cup of coffee."

"Cool." Will headed toward the sidewalk. Charlie and Ben exchanged looks and began to follow.

* * *

CHARLIE PACED THE BUS TERMINAL FOR OVER AN HOUR until the reinforcements arrived. She and Ben took turns speculating about the nature of the book, and Will scouted the street out front until Athena, Sabine, and Marigold poured out of their SUV with a lead-lined box covered with symbols.

"We're going to look very conspicuous if we all walk

in there together," Charlie remarked, tilting her head to decipher the inscriptions. "Especially if we're carrying that box."

Will put one hand on his hip and scrubbed the scruff on this chin with the other. "She's right about that."

"What do you suggest?" Ben asked.

"Have you checked into your hotel yet?" Charlie asked.

"I have," Ben said. "Why? What are you thinking?"

"I'm thinking that nobody will even look twice if you walk into that bus station with a suitcase in your hand."

"Good thinking," Ben said. "I think I have something that will work."

He went around to the back of the FJ50 and opened the door. He retrieved a large duffle bag from beneath one of the jump seats and quickly emptied the contents. "Will, can you bring me the box?"

"Sure thing, boss," Will said. He squatted down and picked up the metal box, grunting against the weight of the heavy lead. Ben opened the duffle and guided the box from Will's arms into his bag. With a yank, he closed the zipper and grabbed the two handles with his palm. The box itself weighed at least fifty pounds, if not more, and Charlie watched him struggle with the weight of it. Then he mumbled a spell, and the bag no longer strained against his hands.

"Charlie, you're with me," Ben said. "Athena, I need

you, Marigold, and Sabine to cast an obfuscation spell, to ensure no one notices us."

"Sure thing," Athena said.

Ben and Charlie started toward their destination.

"Wait," Athena called. She pulled a pair of black leather gloves from the front seat of the SUV. "You'll need these to handle it." She placed the gloves in Charlie's hand. "Put them on. They've been blessed with a protection spell to keep the book from affecting you. Lauren told us you don't know what kind of book it is, could be dangerous."

"Thanks." Charlie relished the feel of the buttery leather gloves in her hand and hoped they really would protect her. As she followed Ben into the bus station, she couldn't shake the feeling that no amount of protection was enough.

Once inside, Ben unzipped the duffle bag and opened the door of the locker. The people inside the station who cast a glance their way, seemed to glaze over if they looked too long. The obfuscation spell was working. Charlie quickly donned the gloves. A thin layer of rust coated the interior wall of the locker and Charlie ran one finger over it and rubbed her fingers together to clear it off.

"Weird," she said. Ben nodded.

Charlie wiped the rest of the rust from her gloves on her jeans, then focused her attention on the thick leather bound volume. She grabbed hold of it with both hands and carefully lifted the heavy book from the small locker. For a moment her head filled with whispering voices, saying things she couldn't quite make out. Her breath caught in her throat, and her fingertips tingled, despite the gloves. Images she didn't understand flashed through her head. An old man shuffled along the top landing of his home using a walker, the toe of his slipper caught on a corner of the carpet, and his walker fell over. His hands grasped at air just before he lost his balance and toppled down a flight of stairs breaking his neck. A lineman maneuvered a bucket truck and over shot the height he needed. The electrical line sparked when it touched the lineman and his body convulsed when 10,000 volts shot through him and didn't stop until he finally slumped over and sank into the bucket. A young woman wept while she downed a bottle of pills and climbed inside a hot bath and waited for death to come.

Charlie quickly put the book into the lock-box and pressed her hand to her heart.

"Charlie? You okay?" Ben asked.

She tried to move, tried to look away from the simplistic tree etched into the leather cover of the book, tried not to see the images flashing through her mind or hear the words now becoming clearer in her head.

20191213011432 Angela Inman. 20191213060214 Robert

Kilpatrick. 20191213140436 Alexander Lohman, the voice whispered.

"Charlie," Ben's stern tone pierced the haze. She blinked and rushed to get the book inside the lead box.

"Close it quick." Her heart beat hard against her ribs and she couldn't catch her breath. She bent over and put her hands on her knees, gulping in air like she'd just sprinted for a mile. "Please."

Ben nodded and slammed the top of the box shut. He fastened a padlock in place and zipped up the duffle bag. Once the book was safely tucked away, he touched Charlie's arm. "You okay?"

"Yeah, I think so." Charlie straightened up and blew out one last shuddery breath. "I just...I didn't expect it to affect me."

"Yeah, that's why we do this in pairs," he said.

"Smart," she said.

"What do you think's in the book?" Will asked.

"No telling. Could be anything really. An ancient grimoire? A witch's diary? That's what we're about to find out." Ben lowered his voice to redo the spell that made the box lighter than air.

"Come on," he said, lifting the duffle easily once again. "Let's get this back to headquarters so it can't hurt anyone else."

"Good thinking," Charlie said.

CHAPTER 6

harlie gathered with Ben, Will, and three others from her team in a small windowless room with white walls and a wooden table in the center. Ben called it a clean room. But Charlie wasn't sure why. From what she knew of clean rooms, they were sterile places, free of dust and contaminants. While this room was certainly clean, it didn't seem very special.

Ben had removed the lead-lined box from the duffle bag and had carried it into the clean room and set it on the table.

"Athena, Sabine. Will you please mark the walls?" Ben asked.

"Of course," Athena said. There was a drawer in the center of the table, and Athena opened it, withdrawing

69

two pieces of gray chalk. She handed one to Sabine, and they carried out Ben's orders.

"Charlie, can you help me?" Ben asked.

"Of course," she said, moving closer to him. "What can I do?"

"Look in the drawer. There should be six crystals inside. Can you take them out and set them around the box?"

"Absolutely," Charlie said.

"Will, why don't you come with me," Ben said.

"You got it, boss," Will said. The two of them left the room.

Charlie opened the door and found a small ceramic dish holding crystals of various shades and sizes. She puzzled over them for a moment. There were more than six. Which ones should she choose? She looked around for help, but Sabine and Athena were busy scribbling symbols on the walls. She could ask. Should ask. Right? Still, she hated to be wrong.

Something Jen had said rang through her head.

I don't know what you're so worried about. You are a natural-born witch if there ever was one, her cousin had said.

Charlie wasn't sure there was such a thing. Although she did believe her abilities ran in the family, but spells and potions and charms? Those things were all learned. Practiced. And in some ways almost an art form.

Anybody could be a witch with enough faith, study, and practice.

Charlie picked through the stones and selected several that she knew. Four black tourmalines, a clear quartz crystal, and a shiny black stone she thought might be Jet, but she wasn't quite sure. She placed the black tourmalines in the corners of the table, the crystal quartz on the front side of the lead-lined box, and the Jet on the rear.

Ben and Will returned a few moments later. Ben carried a small bottle of greenish liquid, and Will placed six small paper cups on the table, then stepped back with his arms crossed and looked at the witches' handiwork on the walls.

Ben appeared to scan Charlie's arrangement on the table and a line formed between his eyebrows. He quietly reached inside the drawer and replaced the two rear tourmalines with two matching black crystals with red spots.

Charlie frowned. "What are those?"

"Black tourmaline with red jasper. To keep things protected and grounded," Ben said.

"Doesn't the Jet do that?" Charlie asked.

"Sure, this is just for a little extra, that's all. Your choices were sound." He smiled in a reassuring way before moving on to more vital matters. "Come on y'all, I need you to drink this down. Charlie, I think you'll need a double dose."

"Why?" she asked.

"Because the book seemed to affect you the most. Even with your protective gloves on," he said.

"What is that?" she asked.

"It's a resistance potion. It helps to make us more resistant to suggestion, especially from forces outside of ourselves. It's just a precaution. The crystals will help a lot by absorbing the dark energy of the book," he said.

Ben carefully poured the concoction into the paper cups, stopping at the halfway point on all of them but one. The last cup he filled almost to the brim and handed it to Charlie.

She sniffed it. Her stomach turned, and she fought the urge to gag at the rotten egg aroma.

"Pee-yew that stinks." She wrinkled her nose and held the cup away from her face.

"I know," Ben said. "I'm afraid I can't help that. If you hold your nose, that'll help."

Charlie grimaced but didn't argue. "Bottoms up, I guess." She held up her cup in a toast, then pinched her nose shut and swallowed the disgusting green liquid. She managed to get it down, then crushed the paper cup in her hand, shook her head, and wagged her tongue, trying to rid herself of the taste.

"There's a water fountain right outside the door if anyone wants to clear their palate," Ben said, looking directly at Charlie.

She took a moment, stepped outside of the room and found the fountain. It was unlike any water fountain she'd ever seen, though. It looked more like a water feature installation for a fancy garden, like in the architecture magazines her ex-mother-in-law liked. The water flowed from a long, flat lip in the wall to a stone bowl with a small drain in the bottom. Various symbols were carved into the stone. That must have been what made the water special. The problem was, she had no idea how to drink from it. She couldn't see a dispenser for paper cones or cups anywhere. Should she just put her hand into the stream? She frowned at that idea. It didn't seem very sanitary.

"Everything okay?" Ben said, coming up behind her.

"Other than me feeling stupid, everything's great," she said.

"Sorry. I should've explained the fountains."

"There's more than one?"

"Yeah, two on every floor," he explained. "They're elemental fountains, and they offer healing, protection, and cleansing."

"That's a big job," Charlie quipped.

"Yeah, I suppose it is." he grinned.

"How do you use it without spoiling it for everybody else?"

Ben stepped up to the fountain and bowed his head.

"Thank you, goddess, for the protection from those who would wish me harm."

He held his hand under the stream of water flowing from the wall and formed a cup with his fingers and thumb, brought the water to his mouth and drank it down.

"You offer thanks to the goddess and ask for your intention of healing, protection, or cleansing. Don't worry. The water goes through an extensive filtration after you put your hands under the stream. Your turn." He stepped back and gestured for Charlie to take his place.

"Okay," Charlie said, putting herself right in front of the fountain. She bowed her head slightly.

"Thank you, goddess, for protection from the spells of others that may do me harm." She extended her hand into the fountain, letting the cool water flow over the skin of her palm for a second. A feeling of euphoria spread through her body, and she shivered.

Ben chuckled. "Feels great, doesn't it?"

"It does," Charlie said. "It's like I don't want it to end."

"I know. If you drink from it though, it'll help extend that feeling for a little while."

Charlie nodded and cupped her hand and gathered enough water for a sip. She drew her hand to her mouth and drank. The water tasted cool and sweet on her tongue, and the aftertaste of the potion evaporated.

Strangely, it felt like more water than what she'd managed to get into her palm. When she was done, she started to put her hand in the stream again.

"Don't," Ben said, touching the top of her arm, gently pressing it away. "Just one drink from this fountain," he said. "More than one sip, and it can counteract the protection you just asked for."

"Even if I'm thankful for it again?" she asked.

"Yeah, 'fraid so," he said.

"Okay." Charlie drew her hand back. "I'm still a little thirsty though."

"Come on. There's a vending machine in the break room at the end of the hall. I'll buy you a water," he said.

"Thanks," she said.

A FEW MINUTES LATER, THEY REJOINED THE GROUP AND began the arduous task of dealing with the book.

To work with the book, Charlie, Ben, and Athena all put on long, linen aprons and then linen smocks to cover their clothing. Ben and Athena put on gloves, and Charlie slipped her hands into the leather gloves Athena had given her earlier. She hoped the water she'd drunk would give her the added protection she needed.

Ben carefully opened the box and lifted the book from the shield of the lead lining. He placed it on the butcher block table and moved the box to the shelf below. Charlie noted protection was within easy reach if they needed to put it away quickly for some reason. It made her feel less anxious about dealing with the hand-written volume's contents, but she couldn't shake the fluttery feeling in her stomach, or the memory of those words echoing through her head when she'd first touched the book.

Ben opened the cover to the first page and the air in the room changed, shifting to heaviness. Charlie had to push the air out of her lungs and work to draw breath in.

"Do you feel that?" Charlie asked.

"Yeah," Ben said.

"Dark books sometimes do this. If they have illegal spells and recipes for deadly potions, they can affect their environment. They can even cause decay of their surroundings," Athena explained.

"Is that what we have here do you think? A dark book?" Charlie asked. Ben shook his head, noncommittal. She turned to Athena. "Is that why the locker was rusting on the inside?"

"Probably," Athena said.

"Imagine what it must do to a person," Charlie mused.

"I would think with enough exposure, a dark book could drive someone insane," Athena said.

"Or allow them to accept their most base instincts," Ben said.

"You're thinking murder," Charlie said.

"Yes, I am," he said. "The question is, who did the murdering? The mother or the father?"

"Maybe it was both," Athena said.

"Charlie? Any insight?" Ben asked.

Charlie considered her vision of the little girl and her father in the hall. Could that man have killed his daughter? Maybe even his whole family? A demon had most definitely passed through that house. Had the evil creature possessed one of the parents and done the killing? If only the little girl's ghost hadn't run away. Maybe she could've questioned the child.

"I don't know. I think it's too early to tell. To be honest, I'm still not certain that a demon wasn't involved somehow."

"Agreed," Ben said. "There's too much evidence otherwise."

"Maybe the parents summoned a demon, and he possessed one of them, then did the killing," Athena said. "Wouldn't be the first time."

"No, it wouldn't," Ben agreed.

"Is there anything in the book that indicates who it belongs to? Or how the Cochrans obtained it?" Charlie asked.

"We're about to find out," Ben said. "Are you two feeling steady on your feet?"

Charlie knew his question was directed more at her than Athena, and her cheeks warmed. She forced a smile.

"Ready as I'll ever be," Charlie said.

"Ready," Athena said.

"Good. Let's begin," Ben said, and opened the first page of the book.

CHAPTER 7

Charlie sat at the kitchen table in her uncle's house, breathing in the delicious smells of the pot roast cooking in the oven, and trying to forget the details of her day. How could going through an ancient book take so much out of her? Even with all the protections in place, that book seemed to bombard her at every turn.

"So, you've been awfully quiet since you got here," Jen said. She opened the pot of green beans on the stove, gave them a quick taste, and then turned off the burner. "Everything okay?"

"Yeah, just a hard day, that's all." Charlie massaged the back of her head and closed her eyes. "Stressful."

"So, is it too much?" Her cousin's tone sounded

cautious and curious at the same time. "Do you wish you'd just gotten another call center job?"

"I don't know," Charlie said, opening her eyes and meeting her cousin's gaze. "Too early to say yet. I mean, I really like the people, for the most part. And it's exciting to be working on cases again, especially going in knowing it's supernatural and not having to convince someone otherwise."

"But..."

"It's harder than I thought it'd be. I don't know nearly enough."

"Well then, you'll learn, right?"

"Right," Charlie said. Her stomach growled, and Jen laughed.

"Good goddess, we better get you fed."

"Something smells good," Jack Holloway said as he entered the kitchen. "Well, hey, Charlie, it's good to see you."

"Good to see you too, Uncle Jack," Charlie said.

"Where's your fella?" Jack asked.

"He had a death to attend to. And Jen was kind enough to invite me to dinner, so here I am."

"So, it sounds like you like your new job," he said.

"So far, I do. It's definitely going to be a challenge."

"Well, a challenge is a good thing. Keeps you on your toes. And it will keep you young. Or so I'm told."

"Daddy, will you get three plates and set the table for me, please?"

"I can do that for you, Jen," Charlie said.

"Now, that's all right, Charlie," Jack said. He put his hands on her shoulders and gave them a rough squeeze. "You're the guest."

"You know, I don't think I've ever seen you do anything very domestic, Uncle Jack," Charlie said.

"Now that's not true," Jen said. "You stand outside with us anytime he's making barbecue in the smoker."

Charlie laughed. "I hadn't thought of that. I guess I think of cooking outside as more the domain of –".

"Don't you dare say it.," Jen gave Charlie a warning glance.

"I never see you cooking on the grill, Jen," Charlie said.

"And you never will," Jack Holloway said, a glint in his eyes. "Too much work."

"I don't think I've ever seen Jen be afraid of work," Charlie said.

"I'm not afraid of work. But I don't like mess. And dealing with charcoal and lighter and all that is just messy. Now, if I had a wood burning oven, that might be different." She gave her father a pointed look.

Jack rolled his eyes. "I'm just gonna shut my mouth right now and set the table. Before I get roped into building something."

Charlie and Jen laughed. Charlie hopped up from her chair and retrieved napkins and cutlery from the drawer behind her.

"Did Ruby already eat?" Charlie asked, referring to Jen's nearly seven-year-old daughter.

"She did," Jen said. "I put her to bed early this time of year."

"You know, I never could get Evan to go to bed before eight o'clock, even when he was Ruby's age," Charlie said.

"And I bet now you can't get him to wake up." Jack chuckled.

"That's the truth of it," Charlie said, laying the silver and napkin across each plate after Jack put it on the kitchen table.

"I'm surprised he hasn't called you," Jen said.

"He texted me this afternoon when he got out of school."

"He's a good boy," Jen said. She placed two hot pads on the table and lifted the cast-iron pan from the stove and placed it on top of them. She took another pot from the back burner and put it on the table as well. Jen retrieved a serving fork and spoon from a nearby drawer and placed them on the table in front of the respective pots.

"Most of the time," Charlie said, taking her seat. Jack and Jen took seats across from her. "He texted me earlier today asking me about spells."

82

"Sounds like you're going to have to keep an eye on him," Jack said. He pulled the pot lid and scooped some mashed potatoes onto his plate.

"Yes, I am," Charlie said, peeking over the edge of the Dutch oven. A succulent beef roast surrounded by caramelized onions and roasted carrots in a slightly thickened gravy made her mouth water. Jen pulled it apart with a serving fork. She made a motion with her free hand. Charlie passed her cousin her plate, and watched her scoop a generous portion of meat, onions, and carrots. Then she helped herself to some potatoes. Charlie dug into her meal, aware of her cousin's eyes staring at the top of her head.

Jen pushed a carrot around on her plate and cleared her throat.

"So, Charlie, I could really use your help with decorating and setting up the bonfire for the Solstice. You have Evan next week, right? He could definitely be a help and I'm sure he'll love decorating and—"

"I'm sorry Jen, I really haven't given it much thought." Charlie stabbed a potato and put it in her mouth.

"Why am I getting the feeling that you're trying to avoid helping me?" Jen laid her fork down next to her plate. "I understand you're busy with your new job but—"

"I am busy. Can't Lisa or Daphne help?" Charlie asked. She sat back in her chair and met her cousin's glare with her own.

"Of course they're going to help," Jen said.

"Then I don't understand why you need me so much."

Jack cleared his throat. "I think what Jen is saying…" His raised eyebrows and stared at his daughter, as if he was trying to will her to finish his sentence.

"I know what Jen is saying," Charlie snapped. "I just don't know what my schedule is going to look like next week."

"You don't have to get all snappish with Daddy," Jen said, her voice full of warning.

Charlie put her fork down and closed her eyes. "You're right. I'm sorry, Uncle Jack. I didn't mean to snap. I'm just feeling a lot of pressure right now. That's all."

"Understandable. Apology accepted." Jack nodded. "Maybe we just don't want to see you disappear into this job is all."

"I'm not disappearing into anything. I have Evan next week, so I won't be traveling as much," Charlie said. "But I have no idea what I'll be doing for the DOL, so I just can't commit to anything."

"You mean you won't commit to anything," Jen said.

Charlie frowned. "Can we just not talk about this right now? Please."

"Fine." Jen pushed her half-full plate away and stood up. "I'm going to check on Ruby." Jen disappeared into the living room without giving Charlie a chance to respond.

"Jen. Don't be like that," Charlie called after her cousin.

"Just give her some time to simmer down," Jack said. "I get it. New job. New responsibilities. New boss to impress. I've been there."

"I know the holidays are important to Jen. I'll call her tomorrow and make up with her." Charlie folded her napkin and put it over her plate. "I still don't know how much I'll be able to help. Although Evan will be here, and what are teenagers for if you can't put them to work?"

"Exactly," Jack said.

"So, what's old Jason going to do without you, Charlie?"

"Oh, I'm still going to help Jason," Charlie said.

"How's that going to work?" Jack asked.

"If he has a case where he needs my help, I can consult. It's not really any different than what I was doing before. I'm just not going to be at his beck and call every minute of the day."

"I'm sure that'll make him happy," Jack said.

"Maybe," Charlie said. She somehow doubted that Jason was going to like it when she said no the first time. "And there's more than just me that he can work with now. Darius is here, and he told Jason that he's happy to work with him if I'm unavailable."

"Well, that's good," Jack said. "Lord knows, we don't

want Jason to be without a psychic. How would he ever solve the case?"

"So true," Charlie said, and then burst into laughter.

EVAN CLOSED HIS ALGEBRA BOOK AND PUSHED HIS homework aside before he slid the book of spells out of his backpack and laid it on the bed in front of him. He took a bite of the ham and cheese sandwich he'd snuck up to his room and flipped through the book. If his mother wouldn't help him, he would just have to figure it out on his own. There had to be something in this book that applied to his situation. Maybe if he couldn't find a spell specifically for winning, he could find one for luck. The book had a lot of spells for luck. But which one should he use?

A cloud of confusion filled his head. If his mom wouldn't help, maybe one of his cousins or even his Great Aunt Evangeline would. She was the teacher of their family. Evangeline had even taught his mom what she knew about magic. He closed the book, pulled his cell phone from the front pocket of his backpack, and thumbed through his contacts.

When he first got his phone, he had entered every number he knew just to have some contacts. It was a dorky thing to do, and he knew it, but now he was glad he'd done it. When he got to Evangeline's name, his thumb hovered over the choice to call or text. He didn't think he'd ever seen Evangeline text anyone. He frowned and pressed the Call This Number option. Then he put the phone to his ear and held his breath while it rang. A moment later, his great aunt's gentle voice answered.

"Hi, Evangeline, it's Evan, Charlie's son." Might as well make sure she knew exactly who she was talking to.

Evangeline chuckled on the other end. "Well, hey, Evan. I know who you are. I am a little surprised to hear from you, but happy that you called. Is everything all right?"

"Oh, yes. Yes, ma'am. Everything's fine. I just have some questions, and I thought maybe you could answer them for me."

"I'll do what I can," Evangeline said. "What sort of questions do you have, honey?"

"Well." Evan brought his free hand up and cupped it next to his mouth to act as a shield and he lowered his voice as he spoke. His stomach tightened. "I was wondering if there's a spell that can help my basketball team win their game? And if there's not, is there a spell that will help make me lucky during the game? You know, maybe to score?"

"I see," Evangeline said. "Have you called your mama about this?"

Evan hesitated. He could lie. Could say yes and be

really confident about it, but he knew Evangeline would probably call his mom. That's just the way she was. Plus, lying was really hard when it came to witches. Every single one of them seemed to know if he was lying about something.

"Yes," he said softly.

"And what did she say?"

"She said we would talk about it this weekend. But that's going to be too late. My game is Saturday morning," he said, trying to sound as sympathetic as possible, without being a total whiner.

"I see," Evangeline said. "I can understand how that is definitely a conundrum for you."

"Will you help me?" Evan asked.

"Let me talk to your mama. And your daddy," Evangeline said. "And if they are both in alignment with you learning a little bit about your craft and your heritage, then maybe I can make some arrangements for you to spend a couple days with me this week, after school."

"They're both going to say no. 'Specially my dad. He hates this kind of stuff."

"You leave that to me," Evangeline said. "And in the meantime, I can always cast a little spell for you."

"You would do that?" Evan asked. Why hadn't he thought about that? He could've just asked his mom to cast a spell.

"I would be happy to help. But you have to understand that it would be a good luck spell, not a winning spell. There's no such thing exactly as a winning spell. I might be able to increase your luck a little bit."

"Sure, that would be great. Anything would help."

"How good are y'all?" Evangeline asked.

"We're good."

"Then why do you think you need a spell to win?"

"Because the team we're going up against is as good as we are and sometimes, well, sometimes they play dirty."

"What do you mean?"

"They like to call unneeded time-outs, or they hold the ball until the clock runs out. Sometimes they'll yank on jerseys to stop a player from getting the ball ."

"How can they get away with that?"

"I don't know. They just do. The refs never call them on it."

"Well, that gets my dander up. If they're going to play, they should at least play fair," Evangeline said. "I'll give your mama a call tonight. You said your game is Saturday?"

"Yes, ma'am." Evan's stomach buzzed. Evangeline was powerful. Maybe even more powerful than his mom. Having her on his side could mean his mom might let him have more magic lessons, especially if Evangeline agreed to be his teacher.

"All right then. Don't you do anything until I tell you, okay?"

"Yes, ma'am," Evan said. "Thank you, Evangeline. I really appreciate it."

"Oh, you're welcome, sugar. I'll call you back later, okay?"

"Yes, ma'am," he said. He ended the call.

A giggle escaped him, and he flopped back on his bed. "We're gonna win," he said aloud. They'd come close to beating their rivals, Saint Peters Catholic Academy, last year. Both teams had gone to the semi-finals and they lost to Saint Peters by two points because one of the players ran the clock out. There was no way he was going to let that happen this year.

CHAPTER 8

The sound of breaking glass startled Camille awake. She sat up in her bed and looked around, hugging her bear tightly to her chest.

"Mommy?" she called to the darkness. She heard something shuffling around downstairs. Her heart sped up, beating so hard she could feel it in the back of her throat.

Heavy footsteps pounded on the staircase. Camille didn't waste any time. She scrambled off the bed and dove underneath it, holding her yellow teddy bear, Banana, close. Her gaze never left the bedroom door. Mommy and Daddy had been fighting earlier. They thought that she and her brothers couldn't hear, but they could. Something was wrong with Daddy. They all knew it. Could feel it. He'd been angrier than usual. Quick to yell. Quick to use his hands in a rough way.

Somewhere deep inside she knew he wasn't really her

daddy. It was something else. But she didn't quite have the words for it. She had tried to bring it up with her mommy, but she wouldn't listen. The door creaked open, and her daddy lumbered in. From under the bed, she could see his shoes and something on the bottom of his pant legs. It looked black. Her stomach flip-flopped. It didn't look like mud or anything like that. It looked like . . .

Blood?

Where had that thought come from?

"I know you're in here, Camille. It's time to come out now."

Her father's voice sounded strange. Far away, as if he wasn't even in the room with her. She pressed Banana against her mouth so Daddy couldn't hear her breathing and so she wouldn't scream and give herself away.

He walked over to the closet, quickly opened the door, and flipped on the light.

"Come on now. You need to come out and help daddy." He rummaged through the closet and growled a little.

The growl didn't sound like her daddy at all. It sounded deep in his chest and called to mind the lions and tigers she'd seen at the zoo. Mommy had said the lions growled like that to show they were still king of the jungle. Still fearsome. Even through the thick bars overlooking the lion's enclosures, she could feel their power in those low throaty roars. The noises her father made resonated through her little body and all the hair on her arms and the back of her neck stood up.

He flipped off the light and didn't bother to close the

closet door. She used to be scared of the closet. Scared of that black open mouth where monsters slipped into her room at night. But now the only thing that scared her was her father.

"I know you're in here, you little shit." He stopped halfway between the closet and the bed. She could see his feet, and they looked like they were bleeding on top. She bit her lips together, fighting the scream building in her chest.

When he got down on all fours and peered under the bed, she let that scream out. His features, all gnarled and angry, terrified her. The growl in his throat grew louder as he reached for her. He grabbed her by the arm and dragged her from beneath the bed.

BY THE TIME CHARLIE ARRIVED IN CHARLOTTE, SHE WAS the last of the team in the conference room. Athena, Marigold, and Ben gave her a smile and a wave.

"I'm so sorry I'm late," she said. "There was a bad accident on 85."

"Geez, Charlie, it's only your third day," Will teased. Charlie threw a frustrated glance his way.

"I know, I heard," Ben said. "Don't worry about it."

Charlie ignored Will and took a seat at the table next to Tomeka.

"So, tell me, Charlie. Any chance that you had a

dream? Because at this point, we're a little short on leads," Ben said.

"Well, actually, I did," Charlie said.

"I don't remember seeing dreaming in the job description," Will teased.

"It's not exactly," Ben said. "But Charlie's been known to have some pretty interesting insights because of her dreams and I'd like to hear them if you don't mind."

Will held up his hands in surrender. "Of course. Tells us all about it."

"What happened?" Ben asked. He leaned across the table, focusing his intense gaze on her.

"I don't know how relevant it was to the case. But I had a dream about the little girl. You know, the one that I saw in the kitchen."

"The ghost girl?" Will said.

Something in his voice rubbed Charlie the wrong way. She threw him a death glare. "Yes, the ghost girl. Do you have a problem with that?"

"Me? No, not at all," Will said. "I've dealt with my share of ghosts. Of course, I've never stopped to worry about their feelings."

"Of course you haven't... because all spirits are the same to you, right?" Charlie said.

"Okay, enough. Just ignore Will, Charlie," Ben ordered. "Tell us about the dream."

Charlie recounted, in as much detail as she could,

about dream. She described the child hearing a noise, hiding under the bed, and then the confrontation with her father. Only it wasn't her father. At least, it wasn't the man the girl knew and loved.

"So, he was possessed?" Will asked.

"I don't know. It's hard to tell from a dream. A lot of times these things don't seem relevant until they are, if you know what I mean," Charlie said.

"Yeah, I do." Ben nodded. "Thanks for sharing. Hopefully something more will come from it." Ben turned his attention to Athena. "Your turn. Want to tell us what you've found out about the book?"

Athena bounced in her seat and sat up straight, excitement filled her face. "I do. It took my program most of the night, but I think I've figured out what this thing is."

"Your program?" Will asked.

"Yes, I ran a query against every database we have on ancient texts, which includes, scrolls, diaries, grimoires, and spell books. Everything magical that we've been able to catalog in the last fifty years. Anywho, I ran a query and it came back with nothing."

Charlie exchanged quizzical looks with Tomeka.

"You sound really excited for someone who didn't find anything," Tomeka said.

"Right, because the text of the book didn't make any

sense. So, I scanned in the image on the cover and did a search against that."

"And?" Will said. "The suspense is killing me."

"It's the tree of life. Or in this case, the tree of death." Athena sat back in her chair, a wide grin on her face.

"A tree. I think we pretty much figured that part out," Will said.

"Athena maybe you could explain a little bit more to us about the tree of life," Ben nudged.

"Oh, yeah, sure. Sorry. The tree of life symbol is usually associated with those who are living." Athena's gaze shifted from face to face as if she was searching for confirmation that everyone was following her. She took a deep breath and continued. "Basically, the only creatures I could find that use the tree of life symbol in their texts are reapers."

Ben stared at Athena. Charlie could almost hear the wheels of his mind turning.

"So you're saying it's a reaper's book," Charlie said.

"Yes. Well, probably," Athena said. "We'd probably need to ask a reaper to be certain."

"A reaper's book is sacred. They don't leave them lying around," Charlie said.

"How do you know?" Will asked.

Charlie's chest and face heated. "I've had contact with reapers before."

"Wow, really?" Athena asked. "Maybe one day I could pick your brain."

"Sure," Charlie said.

"The big question I have," Ben said, "is why did John and Allison Cochran have a reaper's book? How would they even have it?"

"And did they sacrifice their daughter's life so that they could have it?" Charlie asked.

"That's a very interesting point," Tomeka said.

"The one thing about my dream last night that keeps coming up is how scared this little girl was of her father. Honestly, as crazy as he was acting, it would not surprise me one bit if he killed her. If he killed all of them," Charlie said.

"You did say that the little girl heard her parents arguing right?" Will said.

"I did," Charlie said.

"That could explain all the blood you saw, Charlie," Ben said.

"That's what I was thinking," Charlie said. "We need to get some sort of confirmation."

"But how exactly are we going to do that?" Athena asked.

Charlie shrugged. "I'm going to have to go back and talk to the little girl.."

"It's as good a place to start as any. Maybe once you've

done that, you could call a certain reaper that we know and ask him to come visit," Ben said.

"I would be happy to." Charlie got to her feet. "If I'm going to go back to the Cochran's, I should probably get started. Traffic is kind of heavy right now so it might take a while."

Will stood up and slung his messenger bag across his chest. "I'll drive. I know some back ways that'll get us there faster. We can avoid the highway altogether."

"Great," Charlie said. "Tomeka, would you like to join us?"

"I appreciate the invitation," Tomeka said. "But I think I'll just stay here and make sure that the board is updated with all the new information."

"Okay," Charlie said. "Suit yourself."

Will stepped up to the door. "Ladies first."

CHAPTER 9

As soon as they hit the road, Charlie wished she had not agreed to let Will drive. She reached for the grab bar above her door and held onto it so tightly her knuckles turned white.

"You know, this is not the Grand Prix," Charlie said.

Will gave her a side-eyed glance, and she didn't like the smile playing on his lips. His hands choked up on the steering well.

"Am I scaring you, Miss Payne?" he asked.

"I don't know if scaring is the right word. It's really more of a cross between being pissed off and regret," she said, giving him a pointed look.

"Fine. I'll slow down," Will said, adjusting his foot on the pedal.

Charlie relaxed and let go of the grab bar. "Are you

what they call an adrenaline junkie? Is that why you hunt vampires? Because of the thrill?"

"I'll admit there's definitely a thrill. But that's not why I hunt them," he said.

Charlie sensed there was more to the story, but the energy he gave off felt stifled. As if he were a vault locked up tight. The silence between them felt heavy and awkward. She twiddled her thumbs in her lap. "You want to listen to some music?"

"Sure." He turned the radio on and pressed the old-fashioned channel button to dial in the station.

Charlie glanced around the interior of the '68 Mustang. " So, did you restore this? Or did you buy it jacked up like this?"

"My dad helped me restore it when I was in high school," he said. "It was our last project together."

Those words hung heavy in the air. *Our last project.* A million questions bubbled into Charlie's head that she didn't ask. She didn't dare touch him to gather the information she wanted so desperately. Not after what she had seen the first time.

"Do you see your dad much?"

"Nope. He's dead," Will said, keeping it short and sweet.

"I'm sorry to hear that," she said.

"Thanks," he said. "It's a hazard of the job."

"What do you mean?" Charlie asked, her heart growing cold.

"I mean, if you're a vampire hunter long enough, just about everyone you know and care about ends up in the line of fire, so to speak. Vamps are vindictive and obsessive. Which are probably the two worst traits you could combine."

"I didn't know that," Charlie said.

"Well, now you do," Will said.

He reached over, switched the station again, and Patsy Cline began to croon about walking after midnight. Charlie shifted her focus to the window and watched the cars in the right lane blur by. After a few minutes, it made her a little dizzy, and she shut her eyes.

Her purse on the floor began to buzz.

"Sounds like somebody's trying to get your attention," Will said.

Charlie frowned and reached for her bag. She pulled her phone from the front pocket, happy to see Tom's name and the beginning of a text message.

Hello, gorgeous. How is your day going? Do you think you'll be home for dinner? Would love to see you.

Charlie couldn't stop the smile spreading across her face, and she quickly answered him.

I will do everything within my power to get home for dinner. My day is okay. Headed to see if I can make contact with the girl again.

Be careful.

I will.

Do you want me to contact the reaper in the area? If you give me the address, I can have him meet you.

Not yet. Once I talk to her, though, probably a good idea. How are things with you today?

Same old, same old. Story of a reaper's life. I'm going to have lunch at the café today. That should liven things up a little.

Yes. Tell Jen I said hi.

I will.

Her fingers twitched. She wanted more than anything to type the words I love you. But something deep inside her was scared of saying those words. He called her love all the time. And, my love. But they'd never exchanged the actual phrase: I love you. She could feel that he was waiting for her to be ready. She just wasn't sure if that was possible. No matter how much she wanted it.

I've got to go, love. Have a wonderful day. See you tonight.

You too. See you tonight.

She sighed and put her phone back into her bag.

"Boyfriend?" Will asked.

"Yep," Charlie said. Here was the opening to tell him she wasn't available, yet something about Will made her feel a little defensive.

"I figured someone as pretty as you would have a boyfriend or husband," Will said.

"I'm divorced. And have a thirteen-year-old son," Charlie said.

"And a boyfriend."

"Yes. What about you? Do you have a wife or girl-friend?" Charlie asked.

"I was married once when I was young. It didn't work out. Then I met Amy in my mid-twenties. We were never officially married, but she was my partner. If you know what I mean. We were together nearly seventeen years."

"Were? You broke up?" Charlie asked, already knowing the answer. Her senses picked up that his grief was not fresh and raw, but it was still bubbling under the surface, always ready to overflow.

"She died," he said his face a stone statue.

"I'm so sorry," Charlie said. "Was she..."

Where were the right words? Her stomach tied itself in a knot. She knew death wasn't the end. Not really. Not with all she had seen. But Will Tucker did not strike her as the type of person who believed in an afterlife. Her grandmother Bunny would know what to say. She'd have words of wisdom and compassion or sympathy for him. Despite all her sensitivity, sometimes knowing the right words failed Charlie.

"I can't imagine," she said.

"She's still with me, you know, inside my heart," he said. His hands tightened on the wheel.

"Of course, she is," Charlie said.

Silence built a wall between them, and, after a few minutes, Will reached over and turned the radio off. He kept his gaze straight ahead, and Charlie sensed there was so much more to his story than what he was willing to talk about. When they finally turned into the Cochran's neighborhood, Charlie straightened up in her seat.

"Have you ever dealt much with spirits?" Charlie asked.

"A few," he said.

"Then you know sometimes they're unpredictable," Charlie said. "Especially children. A lot of their energy is focused on their fear."

"She's just a little girl though, right?" Will said.

"Yes, but spirits tend to focus their energy on whatever their strongest emotion was toward the end. If they were angry, they tend to be angry still. Although sometimes, they become angry after death if they feel like their death was unfair. This little girl who is scared at the end of her life, and focuses her energy on that fear, could be akin to a wild animal that's cornered."

"Dangerous then," Will said.

"Possibly," Charlie said.

"How do you deal with that? I mean, if a vamp comes after me, I know I can just chop his head off to stop him."

"You don't put a stake through their hearts?"

"I'm afraid that's just a myth. You want to kill a creature, you gotta chop his head off. That pretty much stops all of them," Will said. "Although, there are some that react to silver. Werewolves for instance."

"Right," Charlie said, feeling like she had stumbled into a very dark wonderland. She shook it off.

"Let me do the talking once we get there. I doubt you're gonna be able to see her unless she decides to show herself to you. That takes a lot of energy, and most spirits would rather throw something at you and stay invisible."

"Noted," Will said. "So how long have you been able to, you know."

"Communicate with spirits? Since I was a little girl," Charlie said.

"That's a long time," Will said. "I mean do you just see spirits floating around?"

"Sometimes I do. Usually if the spirit is haunting a person, I can draw them out by touching the person they're haunting. And sometimes I end up talking to spirits, and I don't even realize they're spirits until after the conversation is over," Charlie said.

"That must be kinda disconcerting."

"Tell me about it," Charlie said.

Will pulled his Mustang into the Cochran's driveway and put it into park. "Okay, this is your show. I'm just along for the ride."

"Let me just text my boyfriend to see if he can contact the local reaper?"

"Wait, what? You're going to call a reaper? Have you lost your ever-loving mind?" Will asked.

"I deal with reapers all the time. My boyfriend's a reaper," she said.

"Are you kidding me? Do you have any idea how dangerous that is?" Will asked.

"I'm not sure why you're getting all hot and bothered about this. I'm the one dating him, not you."

"You're right about that. I'd rather date a vamp. At least I could kill it if it turned on me."

"Tom would never turn on me. I don't know any reaper that would turn on a human being."

"Trust me, they would. They're more dangerous than vamps and just as obsessive. If I were you, I would get out of that relationship as fast as I could."

"Well it's a good thing you're not me, isn't it?" Charlie said. She scowled at him and then reached into her purse for her phone. Quickly, she darted off a text to Tom. His answer surprised her.

Give me the address and I'll meet you there.

I'll be fine. I don't want to interrupt your day.

You're not interrupting my day, love. It's more of a precaution. May I have the address, please?

Of course.

Charlie typed in the address. She bit her lip trying to

think of what else to say. An argument to make. Especially after Will's latest assertion about reapers.

I'll see you in a few, love.

Charlie closed up the text app and tucked her phone back into her purse. "He's on his way."

"Here? Your boyfriend is coming here?"

"You'll be fine. He's going to appear human to you."

"Exactly how does that work?" Will asked.

"He wears a glamour. You wouldn't even know he was a reaper by looking at him."

"Right," Will said. "We'll see about that."

Charlie rolled her eyes. "Let's just go in and see if we can make contact, okay?"

"Fine," Will said.

"Fine," Charlie said. She got out of the car. She blew out a big breath and tried to release the frustration of dealing with Will. He was such a conundrum. On one hand, he was handsome and funny, but on the other hand, he was contrary and downright irritating.

Charlie rubbed the back of her neck and closed her eyes, taking a few deep breaths to clear her head. When she opened her eyes, she saw the girl standing at the window watching her. Charlie raised her hand and waved. The girl waved back, relief on her small face. Charlie took the steps two at a time, and when she got to the porch, she turned back to Will.

"You stay here for now, okay?"

"I'm supposed to protect you," Will said.

"I'll be fine, thank you very much. You just stay here so you don't spook her," Charlie said.

Protect her? Where the hell had he gotten that idea? She didn't need protecting from a ghost. She chewed on her tongue to keep from saying something she might regret. She pushed open the front door, leaving it slightly ajar.

"Camille? Are you here?" Charlie called to the house. She waited in the foyer for some sign. Charlie reached into her bag and pulled out the stuffed toy she had found the other day. "I've got your bear. I think he misses you."

The feel of a hand tugging on her T-shirt made her think immediately of Evan when he was small. Charlie turned and found the girl behind her.

"Hi, Camille," Charlie said. She held out the bear. Excitement shined in the girl's eyes and lit up her pale translucent face.

The girl's hand reached for it but stopped short. Her smile faded. "I can't really touch him anymore, can I?"

"You can, but it would take a lot of practice. And you probably wouldn't really feel him the way you use to."

Camille lowered her arm. "Maybe you should keep him." Her face bore a sorrow that tugged at Charlie's heart. "Do you know where my mom is?"

"I'm sorry, honey, I don't. I was kind of hoping you

might know," Charlie said. "Can you tell me what happened? Do you remember?"

"I remember my dad was acting weird. And then my mom started to act weird, too."

"Did you ever see them with a book? It would be big and sort of scary looking. Maybe even scary feeling."

"My dad had a book in his office. I'm not allowed in there. But sometimes, I'm not a very good girl. I go in and look at the books on the shelves."

"You like to read?"

Camille nodded her head. She wrapped her arms around herself, hugging them tightly to her barely visible torso.

"I just wanted to be near my dad," Camille said.

"I know. My son is like that. He sometimes goes places and does things he's not supposed to do because he wants to be more like me. Sweetie, do you remember when your dad brought that book to your house?" Charlie asked.

Camille shook her head. A familiar rustle filtered through Charlie's senses. Camille's face filled with terror.

"It's okay, sweetie. He's not here to hurt you," Charlie said. "There's nothing to be scared of."

Charlie turned to scold Tom. He knew better than to appear without his glamour around an unfamiliar spirit. It should have occurred to her that all reapers made a rustling sound. But they did not all look the same, which always struck her as odd. The one facing Charlie had a definite curve to her body.

"Get out of my way, human." The silky-smooth female voice drifted through her head.

Charlie stepped in front of the child and held her arms out as if to shield her. "I'm not done talking to her."

"I don't care." Then the reaper said, "Now move, or I'll take your soul along with hers."

"No. That's not gonna happen." Charlie couldn't believe the words coming out of her mouth. Will was right. Although she would never admit this to him, reapers were the scariest creatures of all. At least that she'd encountered. They were immortal, and when they set their minds to it, even a little obsessive. But not in the way that Will thought. They were mission-oriented and nothing, not even a living human, would get in the way of that mission.

Charlie fought the trembling in her chest. Fought to keep it from spreading down her arms to her hands, down her legs to her feet. If it hit her knees, they would buckle.

"I am going to count to one, human," the reaper said. Why was it giving her any sort of chance? Charlie held up her hands.

"No. You cannot take her yet."

"One." The reaper lifted its arm in the air, and the

scythe she concealed in her robe appeared in her bony hand. She reared the scythe back.

Charlie squeezed her eyes shut, but she didn't move. Was it because she was scared, or because she was stupid? She would have to think about that later. Charlie could still feel Camille behind her clinging to her, her small arms wrapped around Charlie's waist and her head buried in the small of Charlie's back. She wondered if anyone had ever tried to protect Camille like this before. Maybe her mother.

"Gabrielle, stop!"

Charlie opened her eyes. Tom seemed to come from the living room. He quickly dropped his glamour and stepped in front of her and the spirit child. The other reaper didn't comply and brought the scythe down, swiping the glinting blade through Tom's body. Charlie felt something sharp slice across her forearm. When she looked, there was no blood, but the arm of her t-shirt had been sliced cleanly. She took a step back from the reapers.

"You are not to take a human unless they are in your book. And I know for a fact, she is not in your book," Tom said.

"She is in my way, Ben Azrael. This is my territory. I will take whomever I choose."

"And you will pay the price," Tom said, his tone more

ominous than Charlie had ever heard before. Her skin broke into goosebumps all over her body.

"Why do you care so much about this human?" the reaper asked. She lowered her scythe.

"She's a conduit. And she has helped me many times to carry out my missions."

The reaper seemed to consider Tom's words. She lowered her arms completely, and her scythe disappeared. "I'll give you one human hour to do whatever it is you need to do with this girl. When you are finished, the child goes with me."

"Agreed," Tom said. "I will call you as soon as we are finished. And a bit of unsolicited advice- something I've learned from this human. A little gentleness goes a long way."

The reaper nodded. Her robes began to flutter as if in a stiff wind. Charlie blinked, and she was gone. Tom put on his glamour before he turned to face Charlie.

"Are you all right?" Tom asked.

"I'm fine. And I am so grateful that you showed up when you did. I didn't think a reaper could take a life."

"They can't. Not technically." His gaze shifted from Charlie's face to the arms wrapped around her waist. "It looks as if you are not quite finished yet."

Charlie reached back out of instinct to touch the child and comfort her. But the cold field around the girl, that penetrated through Charlie's back, stopped her. There was nothing to touch. Nothing solid.

"Can you give me a few minutes?" Charlie asked.

"Of course. Would you like me to sweep the rest of the house? See if I can find any other spirits lurking?" Tom asked.

The sound of Will clearing his throat interrupted their conversation. Charlie and Tom both shifted their attention to the half-open door.

"Don't mind me," Will said. "I'm just a casual observer."

Charlie rolled her eyes. This was going to get old. She needed to find a better way to react before she sprained something. She raised her arm and motioned for him to come closer.

"Tom Sharon, this is Will Tucker. Will Tucker, Tom Sharon," Charlie said.

Tom held his hand out to shake. Will's stared at Tom's hand, and a strange smile crossed his face. He let out a laugh. "I hope you don't take offense, but I'm not shaking your hand."

"You're the vampire hunter I take it?" Tom said.

"I am," Will said.

"Then none taken. You are a cautious lot. Understandably so, of course," Tom said and lowered his hand.

"I'm not done yet," Charlie said to Will. "I'll be out in a few minutes."

Will gave her a little salute. "If you'll excuse me, sir, I've been dismissed."

Charlie watched as Will turned on his heels and left the house. He walked down the steps and out of sight, and she probably should've been more concerned, but something told her Will could take care of himself. And he was less likely to run into a spirit outside. At least she hoped so.

"I'll be upstairs if you need me," Tom said. "It's okay, Camille. Charlie's going to help you. And I am, too."

The little girl peeked around Charlie's waist to look up at Tom. He smiled, and just the sight of it warmed Charlie's heart. He looked at Charlie with his golden-brown eyes and winked before he headed upstairs.

Charlie knelt in front of the girl. "We don't have a lot of time, Camille. And I'm sorry about that. I have a few questions, and they're going to be scary. But I need you to answer them. Do you think you can do that for me?"

The pained expression on Camille's face told Charlie everything she needed to know. The girl wasn't lying. She didn't know what happened to her mother, or her brothers.

"Camille, when was the last time you remember seeing your mom and your brothers?"

"The night I heard the noise," Camille said.

"Do you remember hearing anything besides the

noise? Did you hear anybody screaming or calling for help?"

Camille shook her head.

"You know, I saw you in a dream. You hid under the bed because you were scared."

Camille's blue eyes widened.

"I see things sometimes. But I don't see everything. Was it your dad that took you?"

Camille nodded her head slowly.

"Sweetie, where did he take you?"

Camille began to flicker in and out like a lightbulb about to lose its power.

"Don't be scared. It's okay. He can't hurt you anymore."

"I... I can't," Camille whispered and disappeared.

"Camille," Charlie said, getting to her feet. "Camille, please don't be scared. I only want to help you. Please come back."

Charlie waited and listened. She glanced around the foyer, studying every shadow and every cobweb. There was no sign of the girl. She was gone.

"Dammit," Charlie muttered. Tom's heavy footsteps on the stairs drew her attention. "I lost her."

"I'm not surprised," Tom said. "She reminds me a little of those other girls. You remember them? The ones from the woods where we met."

"A little bit, yeah. Did you find anything?"

"No. Nothing but fresh demon dust," Tom said.

"Which is concerning enough on its own. Why are you here alone? Isn't that why you have a partner? So you'll have backup?"

"I can take care of myself, Tom Sharon."

"I hate to say this, but I question that, considering that I had to put myself between you and another reaper," Tom said.

"We were working it out."

"That's not how it looked from where I stood."

"Are you done scolding me?"

"I wasn't really..." Tom stopped. Some part of her expected him to explode into anger, to be like her ex-husband Scott. But he didn't.

"You're a grown woman, and a powerful witch. And I respect that. But there are creatures in this world who are as powerful, if not more so. I apologize if I came off as scolding. My only concern ever is your safety."

Charlie took a step back at this unexpected turn. He never failed to surprise her. And he never met the expectations she sometimes conjured.

"I..." Her fight or flight response wasn't quite ready to give up yet. "I appreciate that, but like I said, I can take care of myself."

"I won't push the subject further," Tom said, giving her a formal bow of his head. Some part of her wanted him to yell at her, and another part of her just wanted to pop him on the top of the head. She balled her hand into a fist and shoved it into her pocket.

"Your reaper friend's going to be disappointed." Charlie sighed.

"Perhaps. But losing track of the spirit is sometimes par for the course as they say," Tom said. "Have you and your friend had lunch?"

"Don't you have to get back?" Charlie asked.

"I'm not in a hurry. Unless you want me to be."

"I think you should go back to work, Tom. I appreciate you coming, I really do. But we need to head back to the office and figure out exactly what we're dealing with here."

"It appears you're dealing with a demon, from the fresh coat of dust I see."

"Maybe. But if that's so, where is it? It has to be inhabiting somebody," Charlie said.

"Not necessarily," Will interjected from the door. "Some demons are actually corporeal. What we should do is take some of the dust back to the lab and analyze it."

"You can do that?" Tom asked.

"I don't know for sure." Will grinned. "But I'll be sorely disappointed if we can't."

"Yes, that would be disappointing," Tom said.

"And by the way, I could eat," Will said, giving Charlie a pointed look.

"I thought you weren't crazy about reapers," Charlie said.

"I'm not. No offense," Will said.

"None taken," Tom said.

"I just figure you and I are partners, so I guess I should get used to it," Will said.

"I like this man's attitude," Tom said. "And for the record, there are many reapers I don't like."

"Well, I'm beginning to think I don't like reapers *or* vampire hunters." Charlie headed for the door, pushing past Will. She stopped for a moment, realizing they weren't following her. "Well, are y'all just going to stand there all day or are we going to go eat lunch?"

"Lunch," Will said. "Come on, Tom, before she magically starts my car and takes off without us."

"Good idea," Tom said.

CHAPTER 10

Charlie's phone buzzed on the table next to her plate. She put down her burger and wiped her fingers on her napkin before turning her phone over. Her heart skipped a beat when she saw her aunt's name pop up.

"Everything okay?" Tom asked.

"Uh, yeah, just..." She held up her finger and pressed the green telephone button. "Hey, Evangeline, everything all right?"

"Hey, Charlie. Everything's going well, thank you."

"Good." Charlie relaxed. "That's a relief."

"I do have a strange request for you, though."

"Okay, how can I help?" Charlie said.

"Evan called me."

"My Evan?" Charlie asked.

"Yes, sweetie, your Evan," Evangeline said, with a hint of sarcasm in her tone. Charlie's face heated. Of course, it was her son, Evan, and not his namesake, her father, who had died when Charlie was a child.

"Is he all right?"

"Oh, he's fine. He just wanted to know if I could help him with a spell."

"Oh, good goddess, I'm sorry he bothered you with that, Evangeline. I told him he would have to wait to practice spells until he's at my house next week."

"Yes, that's what he said. But he also mentioned a big game Saturday."

"Yes," Charlie said. "Tom and I are going to watch. I'm sure they'll play just fine without any sort of magical intervention."

"It seems really important to him, and I thought it might actually be a good beginning lesson for his craft."

"You do? I thought I would start him off with some of the basics."

"We'd go over some basics of course. Intention, best practices, that sort of thing. I have done this before, you know," Evangeline reminded her.

"Of course. I didn't mean to imply you hadn't," Charlie said. "You'd have to pick him up after school and take him home. I can guarantee you, Scott won't lift a finger."

"That's no problem. I opened the shop this morning,

so I'm leaving right after the lunch rush is done," Evangeline said.

"Let me give Scott a call really quick and make sure it's okay with him. Can I text you back?"

"Of course," Evangeline said. The line disconnected, and Charlie whipped off a quick note to her ex. She watched the screen for a moment. If he was with a patient or at the hospital delivering a baby, it might be a while before she heard back.

"Sorry about that," Charlie said, laying her phone face up next to her plate. "Kid stuff." She picked up her burger and took another bite.

"Is Evan okay?" Tom asked.

"He's fine. He's just a willful teenager, that's all," Charlie said.

"How old's your son again?" Will asked. He popped the last bite of a fry into his mouth.

"Thirteen. He's got a big game on Saturday, and he wants to win badly enough to consider magic."

"What's wrong with that? If I could do magic, I'd use it all the time," Will said.

"There are consequences to using magic. He needs to learn that first before he learns anything else," Charlie said.

"Doesn't everything have consequences?" Will said wryly.

"Of course," Charlie said. "But most things can't get

you killed if you do it the wrong way, or worse, hurt someone else." She dialed Scott's number and put her phone to her ear.

"Charlie?" Scott answered. It surprised her that he picked up at all. Especially since he was working. She expected to leave a message. Actually, hoped to leave a message might be a better way of putting it.

"Hey, Scott," Charlie said. "I need to talk to you about something. Did you see my text?"

"I did. I just haven't had a chance to respond. Is everything all right?" Scott asked. Something in his softened tone made her wary. Leaving Scott had been much easier for her, in some ways, than it had been for him. And now that he had broken up with his girlfriend, she sensed in his voice that longing he sometimes seemed to have for her and a way of life that was comfortable for him.

"Everything's fine," she said. "It's about Evan. You remember my Aunt Evangeline?"

"Of course," Scott said.

"Well, she's asked if she could spend some time with Evan one on one."

"Can she not do that during your week?"

"Of course she can. But Evan has requested to spend time with her this week."

"He didn't mention anything to me," Scott said. "Why does he want to spend time with your aunt?"

"Because, technically, she is the leader of our coven,

and he wants to learn more about his magical heritage and how to perform spells."

Scott grew quiet on the other end of the phone, which did not bode well for Evan. She could almost hear the cogs of Scott's mind spinning, going over the last time he'd been exposed to a spell. It had basically ruined his life. It had revealed that his girlfriend, Heather, didn't really love him, and led to a bout of depression that Charlie wasn't certain he was over yet. And she wasn't sure what made her more nervous: the fact that he was so quiet, or the fact that he didn't explode immediately in proper Scott fashion.

"You still there?" Charlie asked.

"I am," he said, in a low voice full of gravel and reflection.

"Listen, Scott, if you don't want Evan practicing witchcraft—"

"I don't think I could stop him even if I wanted to. It's like you said, it's part of who he is," Scott said.

"That's true," she said.

"And I fear if I try to stop him, I'll lose him." The words *like I lost you* seemed to transfer from his head to hers with too much ease.

"If anybody's going to teach him the right way to do things, the moral way to do things, trust me, it would be Evangeline. If that's what you're worried about."

"I'm not really concerned about that," Scott said. "I

know that you'll ensure he knows the moral dilemmas he'll face. And how to handle them. "

"What is it then? I can hear it in your voice. You're worried about something," Charlie said.

"He's so different from me," Scott said.

"He's not that different," Charlie said to reassure him. "He has your pig-headedness. That's for sure." She laughed.

"Gee thanks, Charlie," Scott said, clearly not amused.

"He also has your determination. Which is a very admirable quality when it's not being used to manipulate people to get what he wants."

"Why give into him if you think he's manipulating you?" Scott said.

"Because he's going to do it anyway. And if he's going to practice magic, he's going to need guidance. Otherwise, it could be disastrous and dangerous. And trust me, Evangeline will set the rules. She's no-nonsense. If she feels like he's using his natural-born talents for the wrong reasons, she will bind him up and make sure that he can't practice anything on his own."

"She can do that?" Scott said.

"Yes. It's not permanent or anything, but, absolutely, she could clip his magic wings, so to speak, if he does not follow the rules," Charlie said.

"When does she want to start?" Scott asked.

"This afternoon," Charlie said warily. She cringed and waited for his response.

"Fine," Scott said.

"Really?" Charlie asked.

"Contrary to what you may believe, I am not an unreasonable human being," Scott said.

"Well, I'm not going to argue with you," Charlie said. "Is it okay if she picks him up from school?"

"Sure. If he's going to eat dinner with her or you, I would appreciate a text to let me know," Scott said. "That way I can let my housekeeper Cora know."

"Why don't you plan on it then," Charlie said. "He can just have supper with me and Evangeline, and I'll bring him home after."

"Okay. Just make sure he does his homework, too. He can't slack on schoolwork," Scott said.

"Agreed," Charlie said. "Thank you. I appreciate your..." A sly grin crossed her lips. "Reasonableness."

"You're very funny, Charlie. I'll see you later."

"See you later," Charlie said.

She quickly ended the call and jotted off the text to Evangeline. Evan would be thrilled.

"You know, if I talked to my ex the way you talk to yours, I'd probably still be married," Will said.

"That really doesn't put you in a good light, Will," Charlie teased. "And there's nothing wrong with being a little bit amicable with your ex. Especially when there's a child involved."

She quickly composed another text — this one to Evan.

I know what you did.

Who dis?

Very funny, young man. Are you trying to make me change my mind?

No, ma'am. Change your mind about what?

Evangeline is going to pick you up at 3 PM sharp in front of school. You can work with her for 2 hours on a spell to help you with your game on Sat. Then you have to do your homework. I should be home around 6 and the 3 of us will have dinner."

OMG thank you so much! You are the best mom ever.

You need to make sure that you listen to everything Evangeline says. And any rules she sets you follow them. Do you understand?

Yes ma'am.

If you break the rules Evan, I will make sure she binds up your magic until you are 30 yrs old.

She can do that?

Maybe not that long. But with a little help from the coven, she could
bind your talents for a period of time.

Okay. I promise I'll be good.

Good. Have fun. Listen to what Evangeline says. And be

careful. I love you.

Love you too mom.

Charlie tucked her phone into her bag and shook out her hand. Her arm ached a little from the contact with the reaper's scythe.

"You're a good mom. Reminds me a little bit of my dad," Will said.

"Thank you." Charlie wrapped her hand around her forearm and rubbed it. A chill traveled up her arm, and she shivered.

"Charlie?" Tom asked, his gaze on her arm and the way she held it. "Are you all right?"

"I'm fine. My arm's a little cold and achy." She glanced around for an air-conditioning vent but found none.

"Your shirt's torn," Tom said, reaching for her arm. Charlie noticed Will studying them and turned more toward Tom to try and block Will's negative energy.

Tom gently took her wrist and pushed up her sleeve. The grim look on his face worried her.

"Does this hurt?" He barely grazed the skin of her forearm, and she almost jumped out of her skin from the icy, hot pain. Instinctively, she jerked her arm away from him and cradled it against her chest. Tom steadied his gaze on her, paralyzing her.

"Charlie, did the reaper's blade touch you?"

"I..." She tried to remember. It had all happened so fast. "I don't know. Maybe. I remember you stepping in

front of me, and the scythe slicing through you and..."
Her eyes widened and she took in a sharp breath. "And
an icy pain."

"Oh, my love," Tom muttered. "We have to get you
back to the DOL."

Charlie hugged her arm tighter. "Why? What's
happening to me?"

Tom's Adam's apple bobbed up and down — a human
reaction. Something he must've picked up along the way.
It was the small things like this that made her sometimes
forget what a dangerous creature he actually was.

"Tom, tell me," she said, fighting the flutter of panic
spreading through her chest.

"A reaper's blade is deadly to a human being."

"I don't understand." Charlie's ears buzzed and her
heart drummed against her ribs so hard she thought it
might beat out of her chest. "What are you trying to say?"

"She's dying. Right?" Will's matter-of-fact twang cut
through the cloud of smog building in her brain.

"Stop it," she snapped, directing her comment to Will.
"Just stop it. I know you don't like him—"

"Charlie, he's right," Tom said, his voice so gentle it
made her heart break a little. "But... there may be a way
to stop it. We need to talk to Ben."

Will grabbed the check from the corner of the table
and rose to his feet. "I'm driving."

Tom nodded and helped Charlie to her feet.

CHAPTER 11

Sometimes, Evan thought he would burst because he couldn't talk about being a witch. Not even to his best friend. It was one of the rules his mom set. He knew it was more for his good than anything else, but man, it was hard.

"Hey Ev."

"Hey, Connor," Evan said.

"You're not walking home?"

"Not today. My aunt's picking me up."

"Cool. Can I copy your Algebra homework?"

"You know, Connor, you need to learn the stuff on your own," Evan said.

"Yeah, I know. You're right. Can I copy?"

Evan scowled. "Fine."

"Cool," Connor said and waved. "I'll see you tomorrow."

"See you tomorrow," Evan said.

Evan sat on the bench near the front doors of Daniel Island Preparatory School. He couldn't believe his luck. Somehow his aunt had convinced his mom to let her teach him magic. Evangeline had even offered a spell to help his team win their game Saturday. He wasn't quite sure how powerful Evangeline was. His mom had never really explained that to him.

He flipped through the spell book on his lap. There were only two ingredients needed for the potion he had discovered that would grant all drinkers of it the luckiest day of their lives. He would ask about it when she came to pick him up.

Evangeline was one of the few adults he knew who wouldn't lie to him. She seemed so open to teaching him; maybe she would help him get the ingredients. Then, he could make the potion and hand it out to his teammates before the game to ensure their win. They would be unstoppable. The championship would be in their pocket.

"Hey, Evan," a familiar voice said. Evan turned to find Rachel Klein standing nearby. He quickly closed the spell book and shoved it into his backpack before looking her in the eye and smiling. "Hey, Rach. How's it going?"

Her long, straight, brown hair hung in a sheet. She flipped her hair over her shoulders and sat down next to Evan on the bench. She shrugged in her Rachel way – mostly nonchalant, like she couldn't care less. Evan knew her, had known her since kindergarten, and there was nothing nonchalant in anything Rachel Klein did. She might look cool and put together on the outside, but he'd seen her cry behind the gym after Wyatt French told her she had a big nose and no boy would ever find her attractive.

She wasn't exactly popular, but she wasn't unpopular either, not that Evan cared about any of that stuff. He didn't. He didn't have to. He was a rich kid from an old family, and he knew it. Knew that it protected him. Knew it gave him plenty of street cred to befriend whoever he wanted in the school.

Once upon a time, Rachel's mom had been friends with his mom, but since The Divorce, (which is how he always thought of his parent's split), things had been different with Rachel. They were still friends, but they didn't see each other as much. And then, middle school happened. They rarely had the same classes.

"How come you're not walking home?" Rachel asked.

"My aunt is picking me up."

"Lita?" Rachel asked, with surprise in her voice.

"No," Evan said. He almost never saw his dad's sister

and her husband, except maybe at holidays at his grand-mother's house. "My Aunt Evangeline. Actually, she's really my mom's aunt, but she's still my aunt, too, I guess," he said.

"So she's your great aunt."

"Right," he said.

"Cool." Rachel tucked her long dark hair behind her ears. "Are you getting psyched about the game Saturday?"

"Oh, yeah. We're gonna win," Evan said. "My aunt's going to help me."

Rachel gave him a questioning expression. "Is she like a basketball coach or something?"

"More like a..." He tried to think of some cool name for her. He remembered something he'd heard his dad's ex-girlfriend say. "More like a life coach. She's really good at helping you get your head straight. You know what I mean?"

"Sure," Rachel said.

In the distance, a small white truck appeared and made its way toward the circular drop-off in front of the school. He stood up and slung his backpack over one shoulder. "I gotta go. See ya later."

Rachel gave him an awkward smile. He hadn't even noticed that she had new braces on her teeth. "See you tomorrow."

"Sure. Tomorrow." He headed toward the curb and

gave Rachel one last wave before he climbed into the cab of his aunt's truck.

"Hey, Evan," Evangeline said.

"Hey," he said, trying not to sound too excited.

"I'm so glad we're getting to spend some time together."

"Yeah, me too," he said. "I'm really glad you called my mom."

"Me too," she said. "This is a real treat."

Evangeline's sharp blue eyes looked past him, her stare landing on Rachel.

"Does your friend need a ride?"

"No. Her mom is..." He thought about the best way to say it so as not to upset his aunt. Rachel's mom could be flakey and forgetful. "I'm sure her mom is on her way."

"Maybe we should check with her. Just in case." Evangeline shifted her gaze to him. He squirmed beneath the weight of it.

"I've known her since kindergarten. Her mom's late sometimes, but she never forgets."

"Maybe we should wait with her," Evangeline suggested.

"Are you..." Evan hesitated. Being a witch meant trusting your intuition. He'd done it his whole life without even realizing he was doing it. Maybe his aunt sensed something about Rachel. "Is she... okay?"

Evangeline's gaze shifted back to Rachel, and a wide smile brightened his aunt's face. "Oh yes, she's fine. But the mama in me doesn't like to see a child standing out there all alone. Makes my danger alarm go off. You know what I mean?"

"Yeah." He glanced at his friend sitting on the bench, entranced by the phone in her hand. A worried frown marred her young face, and for a second, his heart skipped a beat. Her mother wasn't coming. He didn't know how he knew that. He just knew it. He rolled down the window.

"Hey, Rach? You need a ride home?"

She glanced up from her phone with a strange expression on her face. She rose from the bench and slung her backpack over her shoulder. When she approached the window, a relieved smile crossed her lips.

"How do you always do that?"

"Do what?"

"Come to my rescue," she said.

Evan's cheeks heated. "I do?"

"Yeah, you do. My mom just bailed on me. She's in Columbia with her latest boyfriend. Told me to take an Uber home." Her usual nonchalance dissipated just long enough for disgust to slip into her voice. "Whatever. A ride would be great. Thank you."

Evangeline waved and said, "You can think of me as your Uber today. Hi, I'm Evangeline, Evan's aunt."

"I'm Rachel. Are you sure it's no trouble?"

"Absolutely, sure." Evangeline nudged Evan's arm. "Honey, why don't you move to the jump seat in the back and let Rachel sit up front."

Evan nodded. "Sure thing."

Once Rachel was buckled into the front seat, Evangeline put the truck in gear.

"I need to pick up a few things before we head home," Evangeline said as she made her way toward I-526.

"Sure thing," Evan said. A buzz of excitement filled his belly. He pulled two books from his backpack, his Algebra book and the spell book Ben had given him. He placed the spell book inside the Algebra book so his aunt couldn't see it, then flipped to the dog-eared page with the potion he was counting on to help him and the team win the game.

If Evangeline was taking them to the shop he thought she was, he would need to find a way to secretly get the two things he needed for the potion. He figured it would be easy to slip away for just a minute and discreetly buy the items. He dug his wallet out of his back pocket and checked his cash levels. His dad had given him his allowance on Sunday. So far, he'd only spent $5 on two tickets to the dance Saturday night, which left him $40 for the rest of the weekend. Hopefully, it would be enough to cover any ingredients he needed and also enough for pizza with the team after the game. He hated asking his mom for money. She just didn't have a whole lot extra to give. He would find a way to make it stretch, even if it meant going into the safe in his dad's office and pulling a twenty out of the emergency fund envelope his dad kept there.

Evan sat on the edge of his seat, feeling like a rebel perched between the two front seats. The old truck had no working seatbelt for the jump seat. A linen sachet bag hung from the rearview mirror, and Evan wondered what was inside.

"So, Rachel, what's your favorite subject?" Evangeline asked. "Mine was always home economics. I don't know that they even teach that anymore, do they?"

"No, ma'am, they don't." Rachel glanced at Evan. He shrugged. "I like history. I think it's really interesting. The past. Where we came from. As human beings, I mean."

"There's a lot to be learned from the past."

"I think so, too," Rachel said.

"So," Evangeline hesitated. She gave Rachel a side-eyed glance and turned on her blinker. "Is your mother coming home tonight?"

Rachel shifted in her seat, and her dark blue nails scraped across the fabric when she closed her fingers into a tight fist.

"Uh-huh, probably."

"But you're not sure?" Evangeline asked.

"Sometimes she doesn't. It just all depends on how

much she's drinking," Rachel said bluntly. An energy Evan had never felt before filled the space around Rachel and spilled over onto him. He sat back in his seat and held his hand to his chest. It didn't hurt exactly — it was more of an ache. A heartache. Was this what his mom meant when she said she could feel someone else's heart aching? It wrapped around him, making it hard to breathe for a minute.

"Evan? You all right?" Evangeline asked. He looked up and realized she had parked her truck on the street.

"I'm fine," he muttered. "Just ready to stretch my legs."

Evangeline's eyes narrowed, and he could feel her looking at him, trying to determine if he was lying or not. She smiled and nodded. "Let's go then."

The three of them hopped out of the car, and Evangeline led them into a shop with a small gem-shaped sign of a cut amethyst.

"Evangeline, are we at the right place?" Evan whispered to her once they were inside. "This doesn't look like the place Ben took me and my mom to."

"I know, sweetie," Evangeline said. "I wanted to get some basic supplies."

"Wow," Rachel said, looking around at the geodes on a large display shelf at the front of the shop. "This is amazing."

"Yes, it is." Evangeline sidled up next to her.

"Evangeline!" A woman approached them. Her dark

gray eyes, pronounced nose, and black clothing reminded Evan of the crows his mother sometimes fed behind her house. When he asked why she fed them, she'd told him she'd made a deal with them. She'd give them food they liked — peanuts, dog kibble, egg yolks, and fruit, and they'd keep an eye on her house for her and warn her of any danger. He'd thought she was a little crazy for saying such things, but somehow, looking at this woman with her sleek black hair and nearly black eyes, he wasn't so sure.

"Hi, Magda," Evangeline said. "I need a few supplies."

"Well, you've come to the right place." Her red lips drew up into a bow. "Who do you have here?"

"This is my grand-nephew, Evan, and his friend, Rachel."

"You must be Charlie's son." Magda took a step closer to him. "You look so much like her."

"Thanks?" Evan glanced at Evangeline for support.

"Magda's an old family friend, Evan. She's known your mom since she was younger than you."

"Oh, right," Evan said.

"I was hoping that maybe Diana could show Rachel around the shop."

The two women exchanged a glance, and Evan sensed something pass between them. He hadn't honed his talents enough to pick up on what the two women were doing, but he knew enough to keep his mouth shut.

138

"Of course. Would you like to get a lesson on jewelry-making, Rachel?"

Rachel's eyes widened and she looked to Evan. He gave her a nod.

"Sure. That'd be great," Rachel said.

"Come with me. We're going to find you the perfect crystal beads."

Magda ushered Rachel toward the woman standing behind the counter near the back of the store.

"That should keep her distracted while we shop," Evangeline explained. "And Diana makes some of the best protection jewelry in the state. Which should keep your girlfriend safe." She winked at Evan.

He opened his mouth to protest, to say Rachel wasn't really his girlfriend, but some part of him didn't want to argue. He wondered what Rachel would say if she really knew what was going on here. Really knew that he and his aunt were witches, and places like this one had back rooms full of supplies for spells and magic potions that ran the gamut.

Would she still like him? Still think him cool? He couldn't say why it mattered what Rachel thought, but it did.

"Come on, Evan." Evangeline tugged at his sleeve. "Let's go get what we need."

"Yes, ma'am." Evan grinned and followed her toward a door that had a sign on it that read:

No Entry. Employees Only.

Which, from his brief experience of places like this, was really code for Witches Only. He glanced over his shoulder at Rachel. She bent over a glass display in front of Diana, flicking her hair away from her face to look at the stones.

The pert-nosed witch looked up and smiled at him before signaling that he should get a move on with a slight turn of her pointed chin. He nodded and followed his aunt through the door.

* * *

Dust tickled Evan's nose once the heavy door closed behind him. The scene felt familiar. Shelves lining the walls held large glass jars filled with everything from tree bark to bones, from dried herbs and flowers to stinky yellow sulfur powder. The collection also included small jars with more unusual ingredients such as desiccated insects. Several large aquariums were home to salamanders, frogs, and even a snake or two.

"Magda? What are these for?" He pointed to several bright green frogs sitting in a shallow pan of water.

"Different types of spells or sometimes familiars," Magda said.

"Familiars? You mean like pets?" Evan moved his gaze

to a pale yellow snake wrapped around a tree branch in its cage. He gently tapped on the window.

"Please don't do that, sweetie," Magda said. "You'll upset him."

She glided across the room and stood in front of him.

"Familiars aren't really pets, although most of our customers come to love their familiars very much." Her intense dark gray eyes pinned him in place. "A familiar will pledge to protect its master or mistress. It can absorb magic — especially if it's malicious magic — aimed at its master. Some, like those frogs, can act defensively to protect its master."

"What do you mean?"

"They will kill for their master if it means protecting him or her. They will also die for their master."

Evan's chest went cold, and he shuddered. "My mom has a new kitten. She said it's her familiar. That the kitten chose her."

Magda tilted her head and shrugged. "Your mother's very lucky."

"But that means Poe could die, right?"

"Perhaps. But she could also save your mother's life," Magda said.

"Right," he said. "Of course."

Magda smiled and started to turn away. Evan reached for the sleeve of her sweater. He lowered his voice to a whisper.

"Magda?" His gaze cut over to his aunt, who seemed preoccupied with a jar of dried flower petals.

"Do you have any Powdered Rue or Tonka beans?"

Magda's green eyes narrowed, and she cocked her head. "Why would you need that?"

Evan glanced at his aunt again for any sign that she'd overheard. Magda stepped closer. "What are you up to, young man?"

"I have a spell, a potion really, and I need some Rue and Tonka beans to complete it," he whispered.

"What sort of potion?"

"A lucky day potion."

Magda's mouth opened as if to say 'ah,' and she nodded. "Is your aunt going to help you with it? Luck potions can be very tricky."

"Yes, she's going to help me," he nodded.

Magda scanned his face as if she were trying to determine whether he was lying or not. His mother sometimes did the same thing, and while he rarely got away with lying to his mother, other people were different. It sometimes shocked him how easily he could play with the truth, how easy it was to make people believe whatever he told them as long as it wasn't too outrageous. And what did it hurt really? He would pay her for the ingredients and they'd both get what they wanted.

"All right," she said. "I'll add it to your aunt's order."

"I'll pay for it. It's my spell. And, you know, my aunt doesn't have a lot of money."

Magda looked over at Evangeline. "I see."

Evan flashed his smile, and Magda immediately smiled back. His grandmother had once told him that people mirror what they see.

"If you want people to smile at you, honey," his grandmother had said, "then you must smile first. And with such a handsome face, the girls won't be able to resist returning your smile. You can get away with an awful lot with that smile, just like your daddy did when he was your age."

Magda gestured for him to follow her to the work table. "Are you finding what you need, Evangeline?"

"Yes, I think so," Evangeline said, placing a jar marked Crushed White Sage on the worktable. "I also need some black candles, and that chamomile tea looks wonderful. Could I get some of that, too, please?"

"Of course," Magda said. "I'll get the ingredients for Evan, too." She flashed her eyes at Evangeline. Evan's face flamed, the heat stretched from his cheeks to his chest.

"What ingredients?" Evangeline asked. He'd seen that look before on his mother's face. A mixed look of suspicion and disappointment.

"For his luck spell, isn't that right, honey? You did say it was a luck spell?"

"Um." Evan shifted his feet. "Yes, ma'am."

"He said you would be helping him with it, which is the only reason I would ever sell these ingredients to a minor witch. Because... well, you know how luck spells can go."

Magda cocked one eyebrow and curled her lips into a snarl. "And I don't need the DOL breathing down my neck about what I'm selling to minor witches."

"Oh, of course. Please add it to my order. Evan and I will definitely talk about the consequences of certain spells, like luck or love."

"Okay, then," Magda said. "As long he has some supervision."

"Oh, don't you worry. He will definitely be supervised."

"May I see the spell?" Magda asked.

"Why?" Evan asked.

"So I know exactly how much you need," Magda said.

"Right." Evan frowned, dropped his book bag to the ground, and retrieved the book. He handed it to Magda.

She flipped through to the dog-eared page. "Is this the spell?" she asked, holding the book wide open. Evangeline moved right behind Evan and looked over his shoulder. "Evan, I thought we discussed this. No potions," she whispered into his ear.

"Yes ma'am," he said.

"Do you still want the ingredients?" Magda asked.

"Yes," Evangeline said. "We'll take them."

Magda nodded and laid the book on the table next to her scales.

Evan hunched over and watched as Magda measured out the powdered Rue and Tonka beans into two small paper bags, then handed them over to Evangeline, along with his chances to beat Saint Peter's on Saturday.

CHAPTER 12

The skin on Charlie's forearm stretched tight, and the ache spread from her wrist up to her shoulder and into her chest. The heaviness made breathing hard, and she didn't push away the oxygen mask when the nurse covered her face with it.

The stricken look on Tom's face worried her more than any of the medical banter flying around her from the doctor and nurses. She couldn't hear Tom, pale-faced and wild-eyed, argue with the doctor just outside the ER room where they'd brought her, but she could see him. He waved his arms and stomped his foot.

Will stood nearby, watching the argument unfold, not saying a word, his face stoic. She'd been so mean to him, so impatient. So unfair to him for not being Jason. Why should he care if she lay dying? They'd only known each other a couple of days.

Ben rushed up to Tom and the doctor. The line between Ben's eyebrows grew very deep, along with those on his forehead, and for a second, she could see the old man he would become. He and her cousin Jen would age gracefully together. She wasn't sure though, based on the weight sitting on her chest, if she would be around to see it or not.

A different pain filled her chest. A pain of fear and sorrow mixed together. What would happen to Evan? Would she become a ghost? These thoughts swam through her hazy consciousness while she watched Ben tap the doctor's chest and then point at her through the glass of the small ER room. The sound of the machines around her droned, and she barely felt the cuff of the blood pressure machine as it auto-inflated for a reading. She sensed the darkness edging toward her, waiting to swallow her whole like a whale in the deep blue-black of the ocean.

What waited for her there? Maybe a better question would be who waited for her there? She'd been in trouble before, had left her body only to be told by her grandma Bunny to get back in it because she wasn't done yet. Was Bunny going to show up today and give her that instruction again? Sweet goddess, please let it be so.

Charlie's eyelids drooped beneath the weight of the darkness threatening to take her.

When she could stave it off no more, her eyes closed, and she slipped beneath the surface of the here and now into the blackness of some other place.

THE DARKNESS PRESSED IN ON HER, WARM AND STIFLING like a sultry southern night, only no stars appeared to light the way. Only a sense of the heaviness remained. It threatened to smother her. Something brushed past her, and she screamed, only the sound didn't come out of her mouth.

Or did it?

It echoed through her senses in a way she'd never experienced before, shuddering through every fiber of her consciousness.

"Charlie, do not be afraid," a warm, silky voice said. It sounded familiar but unexpected.

"Joy?" It was Tom's sister. His reaper sister. Charlie reached for her lips, unsure if they were moving. Her own voice sounded strange to her. Louder and internal.

"Yes, I'm here." The rustling of Joy's robes stopped, and she appeared in the darkness, wearing her human glamour. Her sleek, dark hair hung down her back and blended into the black silk blouse she wore.

"Where is here?" Charlie asked. "Am I dead?" Charlie looked around her, her eyes scanning the thick darkness.

"Not yet. You are in a coma. A reaper's scythe cut you, and that's a fatal wound for a human. Now you're on the brink, as the humans sometimes say. Somewhere between here and there." Joy lifted her long slender arm and pointed to her right. As if on cue, a bright white light appeared in the distance. It reminded Charlie of the headlight of a train traveling through a tunnel. It struck her as strange that all the fear and worry she'd felt up until now melted away. She could hear the light. It beckoned her with warmth and safety. Underneath the whispers of "Come, Charlie," soft folk-rock music strummed on a guitar.

"Is that James Taylor?"

"It's different for everyone. Some people hear heavy metal. Some hear Beethoven. It's usually whatever your favorite is," Joy explained.

"It wants me," Charlie said.

"Yes, it does," Joy agreed. "But you should know, the choice is yours. You can go or you can stay and fight."

"What will happen to Evan if I go?" Charlie heard the words in her voice and could hardly believe them. How could she even think about leaving Evan? He still needed her.

The whispering intensified. "He'll be fine," and "Do not worry," were added into the mix of beckoning words.

Her anxiety dulled at the edges, smoothed by the warmth of the light. If she were in her body, and not in this strange place between the physical and spirit, she knew she'd wonder if she'd been drugged.

"I have so many questions," Charlie whispered.

"I know. You'll get all the answers you want, in there." Joy pointed to the light again.

"I know," Charlie muttered. The darkness seemed to move around her, and the light drew closer. "I'm not ready yet. I need to know that Evan will be cared for, and I have to know what happened to the Cochrans. They have a little girl, and she is dead and all alone in that house, too frightened to get to this place."

"Some people will always be too frightened. That's why I exist," Joy said.

"Where's Tom? I need to talk to him." Charlie closed her eyes trying to slow her movement toward that light.

"He's sitting by your bed in the DOL Hospital, holding your hand, talking to you. He's not here, because he's not your reaper. I am."

Charlie's eyes flew open, and she stopped moving. "You are?"

"Yes," Joy said.

"How long have you known?"

Joy smiled, and her dark, brown eyes filled with sympathy. "I've always known."

"So, you always knew that I was going to die now?" Charlie asked.

"No. This is not your assigned time. I didn't wake up this morning knowing you were going to die."

Charlie felt the darkness begin to move again.

"Wait, wait, no, not yet," Charlie called out. She reached for Joy, grabbing on to her hand. Once again, she stopped moving. She pivoted so she no longer had to look at the light. "If it's not my time, then why am I here?"

"Every soul is assigned a date and time of death when they are born, but you humans have free will. Nothing you do is truly predestined. Your actions can affect the date of your death. Accidents. Interactions with other people, some resulting in murder, for example. Or even your choice to take up smoking in your teens. All the choices can change the date."

"In your book, right?"

"Yes. Every reaper is given a book when they're born with all the assigned dates," Joy said.

"Names, birth dates, and death dates," Charlie muttered. "Covered in leather and embossed with a tree."

"Yes," Joy said. "How did you know that? Did Tom show you his?"

"No. No. Tom would never do that," Charlie said. "Could someone take a reaper's book? Someone not a reaper?"

"I... I don't understand the question."

"Could someone steal a reaper's book?"

"I..." Joy shook her head. "I have never heard of such a thing. It would be very dangerous. There are protections on our books."

"So, touching a reaper's book would kill a human?"

"I don't know. As I said, I've never heard of such a thing. It might kill. Or it might just drive someone mad."

"Could a demon touch it?"

"I don't know. Maybe. They're not as fragile as humans, even when they inhabit a human's body."

"Will I remember any of this when I wake up?" Charlie asked.

Joy sighed. "Are you choosing to stay?"

"You said it was my choice."

"Yes, but the body must be able to support life. Right now your body is shutting down. Once it's unable to sustain life, your choice goes away. Do you understand?"

"Yes, I do." The light behind her warmed her back and tickled her neck, still beckoning her, still wanting her. It tugged at her shoulders and Charlie fought to stay put, tightening her grip on Joy's hand.

"There has to be a way to heal my body. A spell. Something."

"All this worry can be gone. If you just let go. There won't be any pain. Evan will be fine without you. And your case will fade away." Joy opened her hand, and Charlie felt her fingers slipping.

"No, no. Stop. I'm not ready," Charlie said clutching at Joy's arm. "You need to heal me. Or find a way to do it. Now. I'm not ready to die."

The light behind her vanished, plunging them both into total darkness again. Charlie held onto Joy's hand with every ounce of strength she could muster.

"Dammit, Charlie. You just made everything much harder on yourself."

"I always do," Charlie said. Joy tugged hard on Charlie's arm, drawing her deeper into the darkness.

* * *

THE SCREAM VIBRATED THROUGH CHARLIE'S BODY, MAKING her bones ache. The pain seared through her left arm and into her pectoral muscles. Her eyes flew open, and she gulped in air, before letting out a groan.

"Charlie?"

She blinked and let her gaze follow the familiar voice.

"Oh my god, Charlie, you're awake. They said..."

Charlie reached for Tom's hand, and when she found it, gave it a tight squeeze.

"Where's Joy?"

"Joy? She's at the funeral home in Palmetto Point."

Sweat dripped down her forehead and stung her eyes. Tears pushed over her bottom lids and streaked down her hot face. She gritted her teeth and took her left arm and pulled it across her body, hugging it to her. In a flash, medical staff pushed their way past Tom. A young woman wearing a white coat and holding a small penlight appeared.

"Hi, Charlie, I'm doctor Pierce. How are you feeling?"

Charlie opened her mouth to speak, but a fresh wave of pain went through her, and she squeezed her eyes shut.

"Can you tell me what your pain level is? Zero being no pain and ten being unbearable."

Charlie moaned and choked out, "Unbearable."

"Okay, we're going to get you some pain meds to help you manage it," Dr. Pierce said. Something in the young woman's eyes made Charlie's stomach go cold and she shivered.

"I'm dying, aren't I?"

"We're doing everything we can to make sure that doesn't happen. All right? I need you to stay positive."

A nurse dressed in dark purple scrubs stuck a needle into the injection port of her IV bag, and within a moment, the pain in her arm and chest dulled.

"No, wait," Charlie whispered. "I need... I need to talk to Joy."

Her lids grew heavy, and before she knew it, she was plunged into darkness again.

* * *

CHARLIE ROUSED SLOWLY, THE PAIN DULL BUT PERSISTENT.
Tom sat by her bed in an uncomfortable-looking chair.
He pinched the bridge of his nose with his fingers, and
his eyes were closed. She glanced around.

At some point, while she was sleeping, they must have
moved her, because she was in a different bed,
surrounded by more medical equipment.

"Tom?" Charlie managed to squeak. She cleared her
throat. "Tom?"

His eyes flew open, and he sat up straight.

"Hi." He took her hand in both of his. A weary smile
stretched across his lips. "Are you in pain?"

Charlie swallowed. "Some. But I need to talk to Joy
before they give me more meds."

"She's here. So is Jen, and Ben. Tomeka and Darius
are here, too. Lisa, Daphne, and Evangeline are coming
today, and Scott's called every day. I've even talked to
Evan a couple of times."

"Every day? How long have I been here?"

"Nearly three days. Most of that in a coma." Pain darkened Tom's golden brown eyes. "Oh, Charlie, I'm so sorry.
This is all my fault. I should never have let you go into
that house without talking to the reaper in that territory
first."

"Do you honestly think you could've stopped me?"

She chuckled, and a fresh stab of pain traveled from her chest to her belly. She sucked in a sharp breath.

"I'll get the nurse." Tom stood up and Charlie tightened her grip on his hand.

"No. Don't. Not yet. I need to talk to you." Tears blurred her vision for a second. She hated feeling so all over the place. She took a deep breath and blew it out slowly. "I think I died."

"What?" Tom sat down and scooted closer to her.

"I saw Joy. I talked to her. Or maybe it was just a dream. It was so strange. So surreal. That's why I need to talk to her. I need to know what we talked about."

"You don't remember?"

"It's... hazy. I remember something about the book." Charlie laid her head back and stared at the ceiling for a moment. Why couldn't she remember it?

"What book?" Tom leaned in closer. So close she thought he might as well be in bed with her. She tried to remember the conversation she'd had with Joy but all she remembered was the warmth of the light and how much it wanted her.

"Joy didn't tell you any of this?" Charlie asked.

"No, she didn't," Tom said.

"We found a reaper's book. Or at least we think that's what it is."

Tom looked at her with horror in his eyes. "When did you find this book?"

"What day is it today?"

"Friday."

"Tuesday, I think."

Charlie rested her head against her pillow and closed her eyes. "We found it in a bus locker. Someone had hidden it. But we aren't sure who. I'm hoping Joy will be able to confirm that."

"You saw Joy? When you think you were... " The pained look twisted his features again. "Dead?"

"Yes. Why? Is that important?"

Tom smiled, but it seemed forced. He shook his head and kissed the back of her hand. "No. It's not important."

"Will you go find her, please?"

"Of course. Of course, I will." He rose to his feet and bent over her bed before he kissed her forehead. His lips tickled her skin when he whispered, "I love you, Charlie Payne."

"I love you, too," she said. "I was afraid before. To say it. But I'm not anymore."

"I'm glad." He pulled away from her, leaving the skin above her eyebrow cold. His eyes glistened with tears that didn't fall.

"Don't cry," she whispered.

"Reaper's can't cry," he said dully.

"Then why are your eyes wet?"

Tom touched his fingers to his eyelashes. A look of shock filled his face when he rubbed his fingertips together and he chuckled. "Maybe I'm getting my wish after all."

"What wish?" she whispered.

"To be a real boy, Geppetto." He sniffled and stood up straight. "I'll be back in a few minutes. Don't go anywhere."

"Where would I go wearing this get up?" She plucked at the pale purple hospital gown.

"Right." He smiled and stepped out into the hall. Charlie could still see him. He paced in a circle and his arms moved about in an animated fashion as if he was talking to someone, but he didn't have his phone with him. She wasn't even sure if his mouth was moving. He stopped pacing and put one hand on his hip. A moment later he returned.

"I talked to Joy. She's having trouble dropping her glamour in this building, so she's going to have to take the stairs. She'll be here in a jiffy."

"She can hear you?" Charlie asked.

"Yes. We have a mental connection. Much like you and I do."

"Oh. Right. That makes sense." Charlie nodded. A fresh wave of pain washed through her. She laid her head back and closed her eyes.

"You're hurting," Tom said. "Please, let me get the nurse."

"Not until I talk to Joy."

"Hi, Charlie," Joy said from the door. "It's good to see you."

"It's good to be seen." Charlie managed a weak smile. "Do you remember what we talked about?"

"Yes, I do," Joy said. "Do you?"

"Sort of. It's all hazy."

"I'm not surprised. I have some good news and some bad news for you. Which would you like first?"

"Good news," Charlie said.

"All right." Joy nodded and moved into the room. "I've done some research and I think I know how to cure you."

"Are you serious?" Tom snapped. "Have you known this whole time that she's been lying here in horrendous pain?"

"Calm down, brother. I did not want to say anything until I could confirm it."

"Confirm what exactly?"

"That she can be healed using the restoration spell from the book belonging to the reaper who cut her."

"Restoration spell? I don't think I've ever seen such a spell," Tom said. Frustration edged into his tone and he fidgeted with his hands.

"According to William, it's only given to reapers who have a tendency to take a human life."

"Who purposefully takes a life?"

"Not necessarily on purpose. It is given to those who accidently take a life as well."

"Why is there no punishment?" Tom said, his eyes darkening with concern.

"There is... but only if the reaper intentionally kills."

"The reaper who swiped at Charlie meant to kill her," Tom said. "She should pay for such a thing."

"And if Charlie dies, she will face the consequences. But this spell should save Charlie and will stop the need for such consequences from happening."

"We must go to her. Make her come here and heal Charlie."

"I agree, but that may be more difficult than I anticipated."

"Why?"

"Because she's not responding to my summons. But there have also been some communiques throughout the community that her book has been stolen. She may be out searching for it."

Tom rolled his eyes and stared up at the ceiling. "She was also very angry at me."

Joy gave her brother a questioning look.

He sighed. "I protected a spirit from her."

"Why would you do such a thing?" Joy asked.

"He did it for me. So, I could talk to the spirit. For my case," Charlie said.

Joy walked to the end of the bed. "Charlie, when you and I met in the tunnel," Joy gave her brother a furtive glance, "you mentioned you had found a book and that you thought it belonged to a reaper."

"I did? Yes, I did. We have it! It's upstairs in a clean room, I think. Ben will know where it is."

"Good. That's very good. I'm hoping it's Gabrielle's book. Which will give us some leverage in getting her to assist us in healing you." Joy smiled but it never touched her dark eyes. Charlie shivered. Joy took a seat on the bed next to her. "Now, I need to tell you something difficult."

"All right," Charlie said.

"You don't have much time until your body fails."

"We don't know that," Tom said.

"Yes, brother, we do." Joy gave him a pointed look. "Charlie, I'm going to suggest that your doctors place you in a hypothermic state, to stave off death."

Tom stood up straight, and the muscles in his jaw tightened. "Are you sure? The book is just across the street in the other building."

Joy's expression shifted from solemn to determined. "Of course I'm sure. Charlie's best chance is suspended animation. The doctors here can do that by putting her in a hypothermic state. You know I'm right. And getting the book isn't enough. We need Gabrielle's cooperation. The spell can only be performed by the reaper who inflicted the wound. You said yourself that she was angry. I've gone to her territory looking for her and so far, I have not been able to find her."

"Wait a minute." Charlie sat up in her bed. "Just wait a damn minute. Hypothermia. That's..." Her heart thudded in her throat, and the pain in her arm and chest squeezed tight, making it hard to breathe.

Joy moved to the side of the bed. "Charlie, you need to calm down. The more panicked you are, the quicker the effects of the blade will spread. If it gets to your heart, nothing we do can save you. Tell her, Tom. Tell her she needs to calm down."

"Darius," Charlie managed to choke out. "Is Darius here?"

"I think so, but I'll have to go see. Take some deep breaths." Tom picked up her hand and kissed the back of it before he disappeared into the hallway.

Charlie closed her eyes and breathed in through her nose and out through her mouth trying to still the panic seizing her body. Something warm and soft wrapped around her hand, and she opened her eyes to find Joy standing next her.

"Keep breathing, Charlie. Keep breathing."

Charlie met Joy's gaze, nodded, then closed her eyes again, and continued to calm herself.

A few moments later, Tom returned with Ben and Darius, her cousin Jen, and the doctor in charge of her care.

Joy took a step back from the bed. Charlie reached her hand out for Darius, and he took it.

"You're gonna be all right, Charlie Payne." Darius gave her an easy smile. "Close your eyes, and just listen to the sound of my voice." A sense of calm drifted through her with Darius's touch.

"Thank you," Charlie whispered.

"Miss Payne, we are glad to see you," the doctor said. He pushed his way through the crowd around Charlie's bed. Charlie opened her eyes and gave the doctor a smile.

"I'm Dr. Penrose. I just need to check a couple of things." He took a small penlight from his pocket and flashed it in Charlie's eyes. Then, he pressed his fingers against the pulse point on her wrist. "I take it you're still in pain."

Charlie nodded. "Yes. About an eight on your scale."

"Your friends here seem to think they know how to stop this. They have a better word for it than infection. Although, it's not really an infection. You know that."

"I do," Charlie said. Her eyes met Tom's. "And you know what caused this and what they are?"

The doctor glanced at Tom and scowled. "I do. Which is the only reason I'm entertaining this suggestion of theirs. But I'm not about to put you into a hypothermic state without discussing it with you first."

"I appreciate that," Charlie whispered.

"There are risks. Big risks," the doctor said.

"What would you do? If it were you?"

"I don't know. I can't really give you that kind of advice."

Charlie searched the faces around her, finally landing on Jen. Her cousin stood at the end of the bed with one hand on the top of Charlie's foot and one hand balled into a fist as if she held tight to something. Jen's large blue eyes were glassy, and the smile on her lips looked forced.

"What should I do, Jen?" Charlie asked.

Jen's gaze flitted to Ben and then to Charlie. "I can't tell you what to do. But I can ask you to fight. And if this gives you the best chance of fighting, I say do it." Jen blinked several times and sniffled.

"Okay," Charlie said. The steady rhythm of her heart sped up, and the monitor beside her bed beeped louder and faster. "Jen. I need you to promise me something."

Jen drew up next to Charlie. "Anything."

"Promise me that if I don't wake up, you won't let Evan forget what he is. Even if Scott tries to bully you."

"You're gonna wake up. If it's the last thing I do, you are going to wake up."

"Just promise."

"Fine. I promise. But you're going to be fine. I know it."

"All right," the doctor said. "This is enough. We need to prep her. And I need to talk to you two." The doctor first pointed to Joy and then to Tom. The two of them followed him out of the room, and Ben moved up next to the bed, opposite Jen.

"These guys, they know exactly what they're doing here. You're in good hands. And Jen is right. We're going to take good care of you. I've got a casting circle all set up and ready to go. We're just waiting for Evangeline and Lisa to get here," Ben said.

"Is Jason coming?"

"Yes," Jen piped up. "He's called about you every day. He really misses working cases with you."

"Me, too," Charlie whispered.

A moment later, two orderlies came to collect her. They disconnected her from the monitors and took her IV bags and hung them on the short pole near the head of her bed. Charlie grabbed Jen's hand when they began to roll her away and gave it a squeeze.

"Don't forget your promise." Charlie let go.

"I won't," Jen answered, her voice shaky with tears.

THEY TOOK CHARLIE INTO A COLD ROOM WITH A WALL FULL of monitors. The nurse stuck the needle into one of the ports of her IV bag and a few minutes later, Charlie's whole body relaxed. The worst of the pain drifted away, and she was barely aware of it. Charlie fought to keep her eyes open.

"What are you doing?" she heard her voice say, but it sounded distant, almost as if it belonged to someone else.

"We're going to insert two cannulas into your nose, Charlie. And then we're going to pump cool air into those cannulas. Once we cool down your brain, your brain will cool down the rest of your body. While you're sleeping, we'll be working to maintain your body temperature with cold water blankets. And we may need to insert a catheter into your leg to keep you cool." The doctor's voice floated above her.

"Okay."

"And hopefully your friends will get what they need to perform a ritual that will stop the spread of this... " He sighed. "Infection."

"It's okay. You can call it what it is. Death," Charlie said in a dreamy voice.

"I'm gonna stick with infection for now, and you're going to sleep. You understand?"

"Yes, sir," Charlie whispered. "Just don't leave me there."

"I will do my best. You just don't walk into any bright lights. Okay?" the doctor said.

"Deal," Charlie said.

CHAPTER 13

B en held out his arms, and Jen threw herself against him. He held her tight for a moment, unsure what to say. There were no promises he could make that Charlie would live through any of this. Nothing about this week had gone as he'd thought it would. The needling fear at the back of his throat, threatening to choke him, wouldn't let him quite grab onto the hope of Tom and Joy's crazy scheme.

"I feel so petty." Jen sniffled against his chest. "I pushed her so hard about helping out with Yule. She kept trying to tell me how stressed she was, how she didn't have time, but I didn't want to hear it."

"Babe, Charlie's going to be fine," Ben said.

"I know. I just thought if she was decorating the tree

with us and helping out with the solstice feast, it would make her feel a part of things."

"She's a part of things," Ben reassured her.

"I know it's stupid, but it felt a little like this job is taking her away from us. Like Scott took her away from us. I just didn't want to lose her and now... and now..." Jen's voice squeaked and she wept, unable to finish her sentence.

Ben stroked her back and whispered against the top of her head. "She's going to be fine. We're not going to lose her."

"Ben?" Tom touched Ben's arm. "I'm sorry to pull you away, but if you're going to go with us, then we should go now."

"Of course." Ben hugged Jen tighter, kissed her on the top of her head, then whispered into her dark hair. "You know what to do?"

"Yes." Jen sniffled and swiped at her cheek. "As soon as Lisa, Evangeline, and Daphne get here, Athena will take us up to your casting room."

Jen opened her hand and revealed a small, clear quartz crystal and a black obsidian crystal nestled next to an opaque, green crystal with flecks of red in it. "I've got more of these in my bag if we need them."

Ben picked up the green stone and rubbed his thumb across its smooth surface. He smiled and placed it back in Jen's palm. "Bloodstone. It's a good choice."

"I know." Jen closed her hand again.

"We've got plenty of crystals here. Just let Athena know what you need, and she'll get it."

"Okay. Thank you." Jen stood up on her tiptoes and pressed her lips to his and held the kiss for a long second. When she pulled away, she whispered, "Be careful."

"I will be."

A moment later, the tall, redheaded witch, Athena, rounded the corner and waved. "Hi, your family just arrived."

"Great," Jen said.

"You're in good hands," Ben said motioning to Athena.

"Yes, you are. You have the full resources of the DOL at your disposal."

Athena wrapped her arm around Jen's shoulders, guiding her back toward the elevators that led to the suspended walkway between the DOL's main building and the medical building. Athena didn't look back, and for that Ben was grateful. If this plan didn't work, if Charlie died, he wasn't sure Jen would ever forgive him for involving her cousin in his work.

Tom and Joy sidled up on either side of Ben. "You ready to show us the book?" Tom asked.

"Yeah," Ben said, his lips twisting with disgust. "Come with me."

* * *

THE BRIGHTNESS OF THE LIGHT WOKE CHARLIE, AND SHE knew exactly where she was this time. She turned her back on it, trying to ignore the whispers in her head beckoning her to come forward. To join them in the light. Charlie squeezed her eyes shut, wanting nothing more than to stay in the dark of the tunnel around her.

"Charlie, girl?" a familiar voice called to her. Charlie's heart broke just a little, and if she could've cried, she would have. "Charlie, girl, I know it's you. I'd recognize that light of yours anywhere."

A hand touched her shoulder, and Charlie could no longer resist the urge to turn toward the warmth and love glowing against her back.

"Charlie?"

Panic squeezed Charlie's heart, although she wasn't sure how exactly, since she was clearly detached from her body. She would worry about that later when they woke her up. For now, she just wanted to see the face that went with the voice. Charlie slowly pivoted. She had to hold her hand up to shield her eyes from the blinding brightness of the light. It seemed so much stronger this time. Could she go into it without Joy's guidance? And if she went into it, could she escape it again? Or was she tempting fate?

"Charlie?" The man stepped between her and the light, blocking it for a moment. Even in the shadows, she knew his face. Knew it as if she'd just seen it yesterday.

"Daddy? Is that you?"

"Of course, it is, sugar. Who else would it be?" he said, with such warmth she wanted to curl up inside that sound, pull it around her like a blanket and fall fast asleep.

"Oh, Daddy, I've missed you so much." Charlie threw her arms around her father's form, half-way expecting to fall through him. Half-way expecting him to evaporate like mist in the sun. Instead, her arms found him solid.

"I missed you, too, sugar. But I've been keeping an eye on you, and you've done real well for yourself. Real well."

It seemed ridiculous that she found herself blubbering like a baby, especially since she knew her body was almost dead in a room in the DOL Medical Center. But she'd witnessed it countless times, spirits carrying on with their human behaviors. She'd always thought it was habit. Some leftover memory. But that's what she was, wasn't it? A spirit. She couldn't have stopped the tears blinding her now even if she tried. If she got out of this whole mess alive, she'd remember this feeling. She'd make sure to remember it.

Charlie sniffed back the tears and looked into her father's handsome face. He still had his blue eyes -- the same ones that matched his sister Evangeline's, and that matched hers.

"I named my son after you. He's an Evan, too."

"I appreciate that, darlin'. I just don't understand why you're here. I checked, and it's not your time."

"I know. I got this new job, and well, it's more dangerous than I thought it might be."

"Your grandma Bunny wanted me to tell you that you need to get back in that body of yours right this minute."

Charlie let out a nervous laugh. "I would love to, but unfortunately, I can't. Not yet."

Charlie took a minute to explain what had happened with the reaper's blade. Her father's face wrinkled with concern.

"A reaper? You ought not be messing around with reapers, Charlie. Don't you know they could be trying to make you one of their own?"

"What are you talking about? Reapers aren't made or born, they just exist."

"No, honey. Reapers are made. A lot like vampires are made."

"What? How do you know this?"

"There are books about it. About all the supernatural creatures that roam the earth." He peered into her eyes, fixing her to the spot. "Sounds like you're woefully behind on your education."

Charlie took a step back and put her hands on her hips. "I didn't think you wanted me to be a witch. You told me to never talk about it. And now you want to criticize my education?"

"That's not what I meant."

"Then what did you mean?"

"I meant... I meant, if you don't believe me, ask your Aunt Evangeline. She'll tell you the truth."

"You better believe I'll do that then," Charlie snapped.

"Stars above, you sure do have your mama's temper," her father said.

"You say that like it's a bad thing," Charlie said, fighting the smile tugging at the corners of her mouth.

"Nope. Not bad at all." He cupped her cheek. "I need to be getting back now. You stay here and keep your back to the light as long as you can. You hear me?"

"Yes, sir," Charlie said. "Is... is Mama with you? Is she okay?"

"Your mama's just fine. And for the record, she's real proud of you, too. Now you do as I say. I'll see you again."

"You promise?" Charlie choked on the words.

"I promise. And we Paynes always keep our promises, don't we?"

"Yes, sir, we sure do."

"Now, Charlotte Grace. Turn around, and whatever you do, don't go into the light, no matter how much it calls to you."

Charlie did as her father asked, and after a minute,

she threw a quick glance over her shoulder to find the light fading and her father gone.

CHAPTER 14

"Okay." Ben approached the clean room where they'd stored the book. He waved his badge in front of the security station and the door lock clicked. Ben pulled the door open and let Tom and Joy pass into the room before him, then he pulled the door shut behind him.

"The book is in the box on the table."

"Why did you put it in a box?" Joy asked. A brief blast of sage-laced air from above ruffled her long hair, but she didn't seem to notice. She lifted the heavy lead-lined lid with ease and placed it on the table next to the box.

"Shouldn't you put on some gloves to handle the book?" Ben pushed his way into the tented area.

Joy looked up. A frown marred her usually beautiful face. "First of all, no. I'm reaper. I can handle the book without any repercussions." Her gaze shifted to Tom. "That is, if there was a book to handle."

"What?" Ben moved next to her and peered inside the empty box. An icy pang settled in his chest. "What the hell?"

"What the hell, indeed," Tom said.

BEN SLAMMED THE PHONE DOWN. HOW HAD SOMEONE stolen that book? It seemed an impossible feat. The building housing the Defenders of Light had impenetrable security. Or so he had thought. He leaned forward with his elbows on his desk and put his head in his hands. How the hell were they going to save Charlie now? A knock on his open door made him look up.

"Hey, Ben." Jason Tate stood in the doorway, a weary look on his tanned face. "I heard you might need some help."

"Yeah? Where did you hear that from?"

"A little witch told me. You know, the one with great big blue eyes. Although, honestly, I think she was speaking more on behalf of a certain reaper we know."

Ben sighed and sat back in his chair. "Tom. I thought he and Joy were trying to track down that reaper that cut Charlie."

"Yep. Looks like they found it."

"Great. So we at least have half of what we need to keep Charlie from dying."

"This isn't your fault you know." Jason stepped inside Ben's office and closed the door. He took a seat in the chair in front of Ben's desk.

Ben scrubbed one hand across his scalp. "I keep thinking if I hadn't said anything about this job, maybe she'd be at home now. Or helping you solve some murder."

"Maybe." Jason nodded. "Maybe not. She wanted this. If there's anything I've learned in the last fifteen years in law enforcement, it's this. We all go out there, every day, knowing there's a chance we might not come home. Charlie looked at this job as law enforcement. Unconventional law enforcement, but still, you know what I mean. She knew the risks."

Ben sighed. "Doesn't make it any easier to accept. She was under my command."

"I get that," Jason said." Any chance this place has security cameras?"

"Yeah, of course. I've got the head of security pulling the footage for me now."

"That's good," Jason said. "I'll help you look through it. What Charlie's told me is that this place is locked up as tight as Fort Knox."

"Yesterday I would've agreed with her. Today, not so much."

"You know what that tells me?"

Ben leaned forward and massaged his temples. "Inside job."

"Inside job," Jason echoed. "The question is, why? I thought this book was supposed to be deadly."

"Actually, no one knows that for sure. Not even the reapers," Ben said. "I talked to Tom and Joy about it."

Jason gave him a dubious look. "So, someone – not a reaper – could've moved it."

"Sure. As long as they weren't psychic, I guess it's possible."

"Why not psychic?" Jason rested his elbow on the chair's arm and perched his chin between his thumb and forefinger.

"I'm just going on what happened with Charlie. Even with all the precautions we took, that book still affected her psychically."

"How many psychics work here?"

"I don't know. A fair amount I would think, but I'd have to ask HR for sure. Why?"

"If psychics are so affected by the book, it could be a way to eliminate suspects. Assuming that your security cameras come up with nothing. We really need to start there."

"Sure. That makes sense."

Jason stared at him in a way that made Ben feel scrutinized. He rested his arms on his desk in front of his body.

"What else are you thinking?" Ben asked.

"How secure is this room where you kept the book?"

"They'd have to have a badge with the right security clearance to get in."

"So, anyone on your team could've gotten in."

"I know what you're thinking, but I hand-picked my team."

"Yeah I get that," Jason leaned forward. "But... And I'm just spit balling here. What if one of your team members was possessed?"

"Whoa. How did you get from point A to point B with that thought?"

"Charlie told Jen, who told Lisa, who told me, that y'all might be dealing with a demon."

"Yeah, so?"

Jason shrugged.

"I've been a cop a long time, and I've seen a lot of shit. I'd have to say, since I started with Charlie, that I've seen my share of really weird shit, and the weirdest shit I've seen is demons."

"I'm afraid I'm not following you," Ben said.

"Demons possess people, don't they? Charlie once called them very old spirits. Was she wrong?" Jason asked.

Ben scratched his chin. They'd considered that John Cochran had summoned a demon, that he may have even been possessed by that demon. But...

"Yes, I mean, no. She was not wrong. There are a few

species of demons that are corporeal, but we keep a close watch on them. We've had no reports of them, at least not in these parts," Ben said.

"Then who's to say that this demon didn't jump ship? They can leave the body, right? Jump into another one?" Jason asked.

Ben straightened up in his chair. All the possibilities wound through his brain. "So, you think whoever stole the book could've come in contact with the demon? And been possessed?"

Jason nodded. "Maybe."

"I don't know how that would happen. I mean, the security in this place is so tight. We have sensors in the building that sniff out that sort of evil," Ben said.

"Right. But remember that case with Gabriel Curtis?" Jason said.

"Yeah, of course, I do. Your friend ended up shooting the guy."

"Yes, he did. When I first arrested Curtis, he was normal. Charlie and the others did some tests. I can't remember what it was called, but they couldn't find any demons around him or in him."

"Right, I remember vaguely. Dammit, I wish Charlie was here. She would know the specifics. What's your point?"

"Charlie was convinced that the demon inside the man had gone dormant."

"Holy shit." Ben rubbed his hand over his mouth.

"Would your sensors still pick up on a dormant demon?"

Ben stared straight ahead, thunderstruck by the idea. He shook his head. "I don't know."

"That's what I thought. Let's take a look at the tape. Unless the demon could somehow screw around with it, that should give us all the answers we need."

"I hope to hell you're right," Ben said.

"Me, too," Jason said.

BEN SET UP JASON IN ONE OF THE CONFERENCE ROOMS TO go through the security footage of the hallway outside the clean room's door.

"Just give me a shout when you're ready." Ben wrote down his extension, and placed it on the handset of the phone that sat on the console table beneath the whiteboard.

Jason gave Ben a short salute. "Will do. Let me know when Tom gets back."

"You got it," Ben said. He left Jason alone to watch the footage and headed back to his office. He knew he probably should've stayed, but part of him didn't want to face one of his team members going into that clean room and taking the book. It wasn't just the betrayal. More than likely, if one of his team members had been possessed, that person was probably dead. And if they weren't dead before they handled that book, they definitely could be after. Messing around with a reaper's belongings was a dangerous prospect. And if he was being honest with himself, he wasn't ready to face the fact that his choice of personnel might have gotten someone killed.

"Hey, boss," Will said. "That reaper and his sister are back."

"Thanks. How are you doing?" Ben asked.

"I'm all right. Beginning to think I might be a curse as a partner, though. Seems like everyone I ever team up with ends up dead."

"This is not your fault. And Charlie is not gonna die."

"I hope you're right. I really hope you're right. I know she doesn't like me very much, but she's smart, and it doesn't hurt that she's easy on the eyes."

"I'm going to ignore that last part," Ben said. "But you're right. She's smart. And in a lot of ways, she's become like family to me."

"Yeah, that's what I figured. Your girlfriend seems nice."

"Yes, she is. She's the one who convinced me to take this leadership position. Stay put for a while. Build a team." Ben gritted his teeth to keep from blurting out the truth - that someone on their team took that book, and a demon could very well have possessed them to do it. The thought that it could be Will made Ben's stomach turn. Better to keep his mouth shut for now.

The two of them made their way back to the medical center. They found Tom in the waiting room, pacing back and forth like a caged animal.

"Ben!" Tom moved swiftly toward the door once Ben and Will walked through.

"Hey, Tom." Ben scanned the waiting room. "Where's Joy?"

"She stayed behind. The reaper that accidentally cut Charlie apologized."

"Fat lot of good that does Charlie," Will said.

"Yes, yes, yes. I know how you feel about reapers, Mr. Tucker. And at the moment, I can't argue with you about that."

"So, why would anybody want to take one of these reaper books anyway?" Will asked.

"Well, they have the date and time of every death that will occur in the territory of a specific reaper. That information could be very valuable. Do we know what our missing Mr. Cochran did for a living?" Tom said.

"Sure, he was an insurance broker, I think," Ben said.

"Holy shit," Will said. "Can you imagine all the scams an insurance broker could run if he knew exactly when his clients were going to die?"

"I don't know what those would be exactly, but I bet Jason would," Ben said.

"Jason's here?" Tom asked.

"Yes. He's helping me go through the security footage for the cameras outside the clean room."

"Of course he is." Tom rolled his eyes.

"Listen," Ben began. "I know you and Jason don't have a great history together, but he offered to help. He has a lot of experience as an investigator, and that's valuable. Anything we can do to get Charlie past this crisis, I will do."

"You're right. I'm sorry. I didn't mean to let my feelings cloud everything up."

"Don't worry about it. So, you found the reaper?"

"Yes. We also confirmed that the book you all found is probably hers. We won't know for certain until we look at it, but it was stolen from her about three weeks ago."

"That fits with our timeline. The more I look at this, the more I think John Cochran summoned a demon to steal that book," Ben said.

"Very possibly. The reaper, Gabrielle, told us she wasn't really there to collect souls. None of the family was supposed to die anytime soon."

"So, she was just creeping around looking for her book, and giving us a hard time?" Will asked.

Tom shrugged and nodded. "Yes."

"Does she know what happened to the family?"

"No. My guess would be you're right about the father, based on the dreams Charlie's had about him."

"Right. The dreams." Ben pinched the bridge of his nose. "This guy could be anywhere."

"My guess is, he isn't," Tom said.

"Why is that?" Ben asked. "Did the reaper say something?"

"No. But the book is missing. If the demon was still inhabiting Cochran, wouldn't it still be locked up tight in your clean room?"

"So, you're thinking the demon is now possessing someone else?" Ben asked.

"Yes, I am," Tom said.

"You're not the only one," Ben said. Tom quirked an eyebrow. "Jason thinks the same thing."

The phone on Ben's desk rang, and he fumbled with the headset. "Sutton."

"Hey, it's me. I've got something. Can you step over here and take a look?"

"Sure. Be there in a minute." Ben hung up the phone and rose to his feet. "Jason found something."

"Great." Tom stood up and rubbed his hands on his thighs, straightening his jeans. "Let's go take a look."

"Do you know her?" Jason asked.

Ben sat back in his chair, unable to speak for a minute. What he was seeing made no sense. The video of his boss, Lauren Coldwater, swiping her badge, entering the clean room, and then exiting a few minutes later with something in a black leather bag, sent a chill through him.

"Ben? Are you all right?" Tom asked.

Ben rested his chin in the palm of his hand, covering his mouth. He shook his head.

"Is there any reason why she would be taking the book? You know, officially?" Jason asked.

"None that I can think of," Ben said. "Tom? We need that book to cure Charlie, right?"

"Yes, we do. Joy is bringing the other reaper here for the ritual. They should be here any time now."

"What do you want to do?" Jason asked.

"I want to find out what the hell is going on."

"She's your boss, though. I know if this was my office and I found out my boss was doing something question-able, I would need to proceed with caution," Jason said. "But that's just me, man. I don't know what it's like here."

"No, you're right. I definitely need to proceed with caution. If I rush in there and start accusing her, that could be bad for me and my team."

"Maybe you could play it cool," Jason said.

"What do you mean?"

"Go in and let her know you are aware that she has the book. Let her know your situation, that the reaper is coming. Don't make a big deal out of it. She may offer up a good explanation for taking it."

"Right," Tom said. "Give her the benefit of the doubt."

"That might work," Ben said. "Right now, it's our best chance for getting the book back, I guess."

"You need me to go with you?" Jason asked.

"No. But thanks. I do need you, though, Tom."

"Me?" Tom said.

"Him?" Jason said.

"Why?" Tom asked.

"I need an easy way to retrieve it if she's got it in her office. Since we don't know if it will kill me or not, I don't want to touch it."

"I can't change into my reaper form here. There seems to be something blocking me."

"Is that the only way you can pick it up?" Ben asked.

"No, of course not. But evidently, my reaper form is very frightening and intimidating. From what Charlie has told me, so is your boss."

Ben chuckled. "Charlie is not wrong. But I think you just being there will be plenty intimidating enough."

"Wonderful. Let's go scare the shit out of your boss," Tom said, and rose from his seat.

CHAPTER 15

Ben and Tom approached Lauren Coldwater's office and found the door slightly ajar. The hairs on Ben's neck stood up. Lauren was not exactly an open door kind of boss, no matter what she might say. He couldn't remember a time when he didn't have to knock. He reached for his wand hanging from the holster on his belt.

"What is it?" Tom said.

"I don't know yet," Ben said. "Get behind me."

"You do realize I'm immortal?"

"Right," Ben muttered. He took a deep breath and rapped his knuckles hard on the door. It opened a little further. "Lauren?"

Ben waited a beat, listening for any sound. The air conditioner kicked on, and the air whooshed softly overhead. The strong scent of lavender and sage tickled his nose. Ben opened the door and flipped on the light. He held his wand at the ready. His heart thudded in his throat.

"Lauren?" Ben scanned the interior of the corner office. Sunlight poured in through the windows, making the overhead lights unnecessary to illuminate the body of Lauren Coldwater lying on the floor by her desk.

"Dammit."

Ben knelt by her body and pressed his fingers against the side of her throat. A weak beat thrummed against his skin. Warm sticky blood oozed from a gash on her forehead and pooled on the floor around her pale face.

"Oh, thank goddess, she's alive," Ben said. He pulled a red bandana from his front pocket and pressed it against the wound. "Tom, can you help me?"

"Of course." Tom knelt beside him.

"Just press this against her head. Keep the pressure steady." Tom took Ben's place next to Lauren, and Ben stood up and pulled his cell from his back pocket. He made a quick call to the emergency room in the DOL Medical Center and then texted the members of his team to meet him in Lauren's office.

By the time his team arrived, a doctor from the medical center and two orderlies had Lauren loaded onto a gurney. Will, Athena, Marigold, and Sabine stood back with solemn faces when the med-team wheeled Lauren away.

"What the hell happened in here?" Will said as soon as the med-team was far enough away.

"It looks like she was attacked."

"Who would do this?" Athena wrapped her hand around the gold pentacle coin hanging around her neck.

"I don't know. We need to pull the security footage and start watching it. We've got a little luck on our side. We have Charlie's old partner working with us."

"How is Charlie?" Marigold asked.

"She's hanging in there," Tom said, joining the group. "I want to help."

"Tom, don't you have your hands full with the ritual you talked about?"

"Joy and the other..." Tom looked up from beneath his thick eyebrows. "They can handle it without me. If you're fighting a demon, I can help."

"We don't know what we're fighting right now. Until Lauren is conscious and can answer some questions, our best bet is just to treat this like an assault," Ben said.

"Fine," Tom said. His intense stare bore into Ben.

"Why don't you go back downstairs so I can talk to my team?"

Tom's gaze flitted from face to face before he gave Ben a slight nod. "As you wish."

"Athena, why don't you escort Tom--" Ben started.

"No need. I can find my way just fine."

"Great," Ben said. He watched Tom walk down the hall to the elevator, press the button, and then disappear inside once the doors opened. A strange thought flashed through his mind, to call security and have Tom watched. But he shook it off. There was too much to deal with right now, not only with Lauren's assault, but also with the book that she took from the clean room and that now appeared to be missing. Again.

"Okay, we need to go over every inch of this room to see what we can find about Lauren's attacker." He sighed and shifted his feet, wishing there was some easy way to tell them the director of the DOL investigation division might be in league with a demon. "But before we start, there's something else you need to know about Lauren."

"Where's Ben?" Jason asked when Tom sauntered back into the conference room. "And why do you have that look on your face?"

"What look? I don't have a look on my face, lieutenant. You're imagining things."

"Okay. So where is Ben then?"

"He had to stay upstairs to deal with an attack on his boss," Tom said, nonchalantly.

"What? Are you kidding me?" Jason stared Tom in the

face, but the reaper wouldn't look at him. "Did you do something to her?"

"What? No. Of course not. I was shocked that she was attacked. But she's in good hands now, and I need your help."

"My help? In case you've forgotten, I'm not a witch."

"I've certainly not forgotten that point," Tom said. He cast a disapproving scowl Jason's way but kept his tone neutral. "But, you are an investigator, and right now, I need your services."

"For what?"

"It appears that Ben's boss was attacked for that book she removed. When we arrived, we found her knocked out, and the book was gone."

"Knocked out? Not killed?" Jason asked.

"No, she's still alive. For now," Tom said.

"That's a good sign. At least we're not dealing with a murder. So what is it exactly you want me to do?"

"I want you to help me find the book."

"Well, that's gonna be pretty hard considering what you just told me. Maybe if I can get a look at her office, and check to see if there were any witnesses. Maybe there's a security camera in front of her office. Is she conscious? Maybe Ben would like some help interviewing her."

"I don't know about any of that. But I do know that

they will probably lock this place down very soon, and I don't want to be trapped inside."

"Oh yeah? That's something a guilty man would say."

"Or a reaper with a mission," Tom countered.

"What sort of mission?"

"A mission to save my love." The look on Tom's face was so pathetic Jason actually found himself feeling sorry for the guy. He didn't know what he'd do if something happened to Lisa, and even though he sometimes had a hard time relating to Tom, this was one thing he fully understood.

"What do you want to do?"

"I want to find that book."

"And how exactly do we do that?" Jason asked.

"You theorized that someone here is possessed."

"Yeah," Jason said.

"We need to eliminate people who had access, and who have left the building."

"Huh." Jason stuck his tongue against his back teeth. "That's not a bad idea. But it's not proof."

"No, but it's a place to start," Tom said. "Will you help me?"

"Sure. Let's go down to security. We'll ask for more footage and see if they have any logs of people coming and going. I signed in at security this morning and they gave me this." He showed Tom his visitor's badge.

"Yes, I did too," Tom said.

"To get on the elevator, you have to swipe it. That data's being stored somewhere. Let's go find out where."

"All right," Tom said. "Good idea. Do you think we should tell Ben?"

"We will. Eventually," Jason said. "Right now, he's got other things to worry about."

"Right," Tom said.

BEN STALKED DOWN THE HALLWAY TO THE EMERGENCY clinic where the medics had taken Lauren. The image of her taking the book played over and over in his head. Had she been possessed, too? If so, he needed to warn the medical staff so they could be on the lookout for signs and do the right thing — exorcise the damn thing and send it packing, or maybe capture it and put it into cold storage.

"Hey, boss," Will said somewhere behind him. "Hey, wait up."

Ben didn't slow down until Will's hand touched his shoulder. Ben rounded on Will, and they stood toe-to-toe, Will meeting Ben's eyes.

"What? I've got to go interview my boss to see what the hell is going on around here."

"I know, boss. Let me go with you."

"You don't even know her," Ben said.

"Exactly. I might see something you don't because of your relationship with her," Will said. "Even a dolt like me can see how pissed you are. That kind of shit can cloud your judgment. You're only gonna have one shot at this. I know you, Ben. You're gonna wanna get this right."

Ben sighed and let go of some of his frustration. Will was right. The anger boiling inside his chest right now could screw things up if he wasn't careful.

"Fine, you can come with me. But I'll be asking the hard questions. Got it?"

"Got it, chief." Will gave him a little salute. "I'll stick to asking the easy questions."

A few minutes later, outside the glassed-in room of the Emergency Center where the nurse had directed them to Lauren, they found the door wide open and a curtain hanging from the ceiling pulled partly around the bed.

"Knock, knock," Ben said, knocking lightly on the door.

"Come in," Lauren called from behind the curtain. She hadn't lost her usual curt manner. Ben peered around the curtain at Lauren, propped up on a mountain of pillows. Her usually perfectly coifed, chestnut hair looked stringy where the blood had dried. Stitches had zippered closed the nasty cut on her forehead, turning the skin around it an angry red. A large knot had begun to swell beneath the cut, and by tomorrow morning, Ben had no doubt it would grow to the size of a goose egg.

Ben sucked air in through his teeth and pointed to her wound. "That looks pretty painful."

Lauren brushed her fingers above the gash without touching it.

"It's fine. It... it will be fine. My pride, on the other hand, may take a while to recover."

Will entered the room and took his place next to Ben at the end of the bed. Lauren shifted her attention to Will.

"You must be the vampire hunter." Lauren looked him up and down. From the smile on her lips, she seemed to like what she saw.

"Yes ma'am. Mainly vampires. I've been known to hunt a demon or two, though." Will put his hand on the strap of the messenger bag slung across his torso and stared down his nose at Lauren.

Ben watched Lauren carefully for any reaction.

She just nodded and painted on a sly grin. "Good to know."

She shifted her attention back to Ben. "So, I'm assuming that my best investigator isn't really here to check on my health."

Ben moved from the foot of the bed to stand next to Lauren.

"I'm afraid not. I need to ask you some questions."

"Of course. Ask away."

"What do you remember?"

"I was in my office. Looking over some expense requests for the herbalism division. I'd gotten up to pull a document from my file drawer, and the next thing I knew, someone slammed my head against the cabinet and threw me to the floor. He kicked me in the gut, and my head, too, I think. That's when I blacked out."

"Did you get a good look at him?" Ben asked.

Lauren stared into space, her mouth agape as if she were trying to remember. She shook her head. "I... I remember he was big."

"Big... " Will echoed. "Like werewolf big or just regular man big?"

Lauren cleared her throat. "I'm not sure. Dammit." She squeezed her eyes shut and laid her head back against the pillow behind her. "Why didn't I look at him?"

"Because our instinct is to look away when we're attacked," Ben said.

"Or to run," Will added.

Ben nodded. "Exactly."

"Can't you just pull the security footage from the camera in front of my door?" Lauren asked.

"Absolutely. We'll take a look at it. Which brings me to a more difficult question."

Lauren opened her eyes. "What?"

"Why did you take the book we retrieved from the bus station?"

Lauren squirmed and didn't look at Ben directly. "I... I... don't—"

"I'm gonna stop you right there," Will said, holding up his hand. "We know you took it. What we don't know is why."

"All right." Lauren straightened up as best she could. "Yes. I took it. After reading Athena's report, I knew exactly what it was. I also knew that we could only keep it a short time before we would have to return it to its rightful owners."

"So you knew it was a reaper's book," Ben said. "And you wanted it. Why?"

"Reapers' books have some spells. Some very powerful spells. Up until now, no witch has ever seen them. I wanted to check them out and make sure they weren't dangerous." Lauren crossed her arms.

"Right," Will said, his voice laced with sarcasm. "Because the DOL all of a sudden has authority over supernatural creatures that have existed since the dawn of time?"

"That's not why you took it." Ben shook his head. "You thought you could beat death. Because all those spells in a reaper's book — they're specifically about life and death."

"No." Lauren's mouth twisted into a disgusted frown and she shook her head with each word she spoke. "No. No. That is... ridiculous."

"Okay, then maybe you should stop lying for one minute and tell me the truth," Ben said. "Or am I going to have to take this above your head?"

"That's a very serious threat, Ben. One you may want to reconsider for the sake of your career." Lauren glared at him, her cheeks flushed.

"Heh," Will snorted, drawing stares from both Ben and Lauren.

"Do you have something to add, vampire hunter?"

"Yeah, I think I do. Mainly because I can easily go back to hunting vampires. I don't need you, and I sure as hell don't give a damn about my career here." He gestured finger quotes around career. "The way I see it, you think you can threaten your way out of your bad behavior. But here's what you don't know about me. I don't like it when someone exploits their position for personal gain. You might say it's a pet peeve of mine."

Lauren's features twisted into an angry mask.

"And I will do whatever it takes, to make sure that person is found out and pays for it, whether it's my boss or a vampire or a witch. Now, Ben asked you a question. I think for the sake of your career you should answer it."

Lauren sniffed and glanced away. "Geez. You're both overreacting..."

"No, we're not," Ben said. "Now, tell me or I go to the high council."

"You do that and they could tear apart our whole

division."

Ben scrubbed his chin. "Maybe. Maybe not."

"Either way, all I see is a demotion in your future," Will said.

"Ben, please," Lauren said.

"Tell us the truth, and I'll consider not telling the council. Lie to me again, and I will march to the other building right now and call the high council," Ben said.

"You've become such a goody-two-shoes since you started seeing that little kitchen witch."

"Just answer the damn question," Will said. "What were you looking for in the reaper's book?"

"It's all rumor... " Lauren said.

"Enlighten us," Ben said.

"There's supposedly an immortality spell that not only keeps you from dying, it keeps you young."

"Oh my god, are you serious?" Will's tone matched the disgust on his face.

"So, because of your vanity, Charlie Payne's life is now on the line," Ben said. "I hope you're proud of yourself. If she dies, I'm holding you personally responsible."

"Wait. What?" Lauren said. "Slow down. What happened?"

"Charlie was clipped by a reaper's blade during our investigation. The investigation you pushed so hard for us to take, by the way. Did you know this book had gone missing before? Is that why you wanted us involved?"

"There might have been some chatter on backchannels about it. I don't really remember, exactly. Head trauma will do that you know. Mess with your memory." Lauren gingerly touched the side of her head near the laceration.

"Oh, good lord," Will muttered. "You've got to be kidding me."

"Great. That's just great." Ben paced around the tiny ER room. He combed his fingers through his hair, scratching his scalp in places, trying to relieve the headache threatening to take over. "We need that book."

"Why? Can't the reaper who cut her just heal her?"

"Not without her book. She doesn't know the spell to reverse the effects of a reaper's blade by heart. Hence the book! They write their spells down for the same reason we do. So we can recreate them exactly. Geez, Lauren, how could you be so damned self-centered and... " Ben gritted his teeth. "And downright stupid."

"Hey! I might be self-centered, but I'm not stupid," Lauren huffed.

"I don't know about that. From my experience, messing around with another creature's magic or culture can be a pretty dumb move. Especially if you're not involved in their everyday lives," Will said.

"You know, Lauren, I'm really disappointed in you," Ben said.

Lauren tucked her chin and scowled.

"I'm also going to have to report this."

"Wait, you said—" Lauren began.

"I said, I'll see what I could do. This... I can't do anything about this. Someone in your position should be setting an example. And all this does is send the message that it's okay to steal. I'm not willing to turn a blind eye to that. Especially when there's a whole family of witches who are probably dead because of this damned book."

Ben pulled his phone from his pocket and dialed the number for the Internal Investigations Division.

"Hi, this is Ben Sutton in the Witch Investigators of Criminal Activity Division. I need to report a crime committed by a member of my division."

"Ben, wait." Lauren started to get out of bed.

Ben covered the phone's mic. Through bared teeth, he growled, "You stay there!"

Lauren sat back down, looking like she'd been slapped hard across the face.

"Yes sir, I need someone to come to the ER and secure the accused right now. Thanks."

He ended the call and shoved his phone back into his pocket.

"Are you ready, boss?" Will asked.

"We'll go as soon as a security officer comes to arrest her."

"Whatever you say, boss. Whatever you say," Will said.

CHAPTER 16

E van fidgeted in his chair in the school cafeteria and picked over the sandwich and chips that Miss Cora, his dad's housekeeper, had made for him. It took every ounce of energy not to think about his mother or the stupid game on Saturday morning. When he'd started the week, that game meant everything to him. Now, he just wanted to go to Charlotte to be with his mom. But his father wouldn't let him. Wouldn't even hear him out.

"What if she dies?" Evan had thrown those words like rocks at his father. He was no dummy. He knew how his father felt about his mother. Knew it the way he always knew things.

"Hi, Evan," Rachel said. She stood at the end of the

table with her lunch tray in her hands. "You mind if I sit down?"

"Course not." Evan sat up straight. He noticed that Rachael's long dark hair shined with a little red in it. He pushed that thought away. Now was not the time for him to be thinking about Rachel like that. Still, he offered a smile.

"Have you heard anything else about your mom?"

The smile on his lips died. He shook his head. "Not really. The only thing I know is she's still in Charlotte. My dad won't let me go."

"Wow, he must really hate her." Rachel picked up her fork and twirled it in the spaghetti casserole on her plate. "It really sucks. I don't even understand how my parents ever got along. Much less had me."

"Yeah, I know. But it's not because my dad hates my mom. In fact, I think he's still in love with her."

"And why won't he let you go?"

"Because she's not in love with him," he admitted.

"Wow, that would be pretty terrible."

"Yeah, and she's got a boyfriend that she does love so that sorta leaves my dad out in the cold."

"That totally sucks. Is he at least going to take you to the game on Saturday?"

"I don't know. Probably, because it's a school thing. But I don't know if I want to go now."

"Sure. Your mom is going to be fine. I was gonna go. Not that that's any consolation."

"That's cool," Evan said. His cheeks warmed, and he hated himself a little bit for being happy that Rachel might show up on Saturday. He broke a chip in half and shoved it in his mouth. It crunched loudly in his ears.

"So, did you finish your project?"

"My project?" Evan asked.

"Yeah, the project you said that you had to work on. The one where you had to get those herbs or whatever?"

"Oh, right, my project." He shook his head, and his shoulders slumped a little. "No. I didn't. Evangeline was called away because of my mom, and we didn't get to finish."

Rachel leaned forward and took a sip from her can of diet soda. "Does it have to be your aunt who helps?"

"No, I guess not. But it would be better if she could help. I don't want to screw it up. Plus, I wasn't able to get everything I needed the other day."

"Oh." Rachel moved the casserole around on her plate. "What about that lady at the shop. Could she help you?"

"I don't know," Evan said.

"Why don't we just go back there and find out? You know, after school," Rachel said.

"How would we get there?"

A sly smile spread across Rachel's pink lips. She

picked up her phone from her tray and wiggled it. "Uber. I have an app on my phone."

"Don't you have to have... like a credit card or something?"

"Of course. My mother set this app up for me with her credit card. You know, in case she's late. And we all know that she's late most of the time," Rachel said.

"I have to have a reason to give my housekeeper, Cora, for not coming straight home."

Rachel shrugged her slim shoulders. "Just text her and tell her that you're studying late with a friend. And that the friend will bring you home."

"That's pretty smart."

"Well, my mom's not around much, so I have to take care of myself sometimes."

"And it's safe? You know, taking an Uber by ourselves?"

"Of course. You want to tell me about your project?"

"Okay." He took a deep breath. "But first I need to know something."

Rachel leaned forward, her long hair falling over the curves of her slim shoulders and small breasts. She smiled wider. "Anything."

"How good are you at keeping secrets?"

"I'm intrigued." She cocked her head and narrowed her eyes. "Very good. You?"

"I'm very good, too."

"Cool. I'm all ears."

* * *

Evan jumped out of the Prius and held the door open for Rachel just like his grandmother had taught him. It took her a moment to say thank you to the Uber driver, and Evan's stomach flip-flopped when she finally got out the car. He had never noticed how pretty she actually was before. The splay of light freckles across her nose. The amber flecks in her brown eyes. His heart beat a little harder than he expected when she gazed up at him and smiled.

"Ready? I've been thinking about that amethyst pendant all week," she said.

"Is that why you wanted to come? To get the pendant?" he asked.

Her shoulders lifted in a slight shrug. "I also wanted to spend more time with you."

His stomach fluttered, and he couldn't stop the stupid smile spreading across his lips. He swallowed it back, trying not to give himself away.

"Cool. After you." He gestured toward the door. She stopped short of opening the door herself and glanced back at him coyly. "Oh, right. Sorry. My grandmother would say, 'Manners, Evan.'"

"Uh-huh," Rachel said. A bell jingled overhead when

Evan pushed open the door. The woodsy scent of incense smacked him in the face. He scanned the store's interior, looking for Evangeline's friend.

"I'm gonna go check out the jewelry. Okay?"

"Sure," Evan said. Disappointment settled in his chest when he didn't see the clerk that he'd spoken to the other day with his aunt.

"Are you looking for me?" Magda stood so close her breath tickled the back of his neck, making him shiver. He whipped around to face her.

"Hi... I am Evan Carver. Evangeline is my great aunt?"

"Do you not know if she is your great aunt?" the woman asked.

Evans neck and face heated. "Yeah, she's... she's my great aunt. I'm sorry, I don't remember your name."

"It's Magda. Does your aunt know you're here?"

"No, ma'am. She doesn't. My mom, well she got sick, and she's in the hospital in Charlotte, so my aunt is with her. I would be there too if my father would let me go, but he won't," Evan rambled.

"I'm sorry to hear about your mother. I hope it's not serious."

"Yeah, me too. Anyway, I was kind of hoping that you could help me. I brought the stuff that my aunt bought for me the other day."

"I thought Evangeline was going to help you," Magda said.

"She was, but she got called away because of my mom. But you seem to know a lot about the stuff." He lowered his backpack to the floor and dug through it until he found the small bag of Tonka beans and Rue powder. He thrust it toward Magda and stood up. "Will you help me?"

Magda took a step back. "This really should be something your aunt or your mother helps you with."

"I know, but I need the luck for my game tomorrow. I have the spell book, and it has a potion in it for luck. I was going to take it and give it to all my team members so we could win," Evan said.

"And you don't consider that cheating?" Magda asked.

"No, I consider it using all my assets. That's what my dad would call it. We still have to work to win the game. This would just give us a little edge," Evan said.

"I see," Magda said. "Luck potions are dangerous. Each ingredient has to be added at a specific time, and the rituals involved usually need at least three witches. And they can take days to brew."

"Days? Seriously? I don't have days," Evan said. "None of that is in my spell book."

"Of course it isn't. A spell book assumes that you have some training in magic. Just putting a bunch of ingredients together does not make a spell. There is energy and intent that goes into it. Did your aunt or your mother not explain that to you?"

"Sort of, I guess. They always talk to me like I'm a little kid. Like I can't do this sort of stuff yet," Evan said.

"Probably because you can't. There are practitioners, like your aunt, who might have trouble with this kind of spell. There's a reason it's not easy, Evan. If it were easy, everyone would have great luck. But as I've said, it's a tricky spell. And most potions are meant for the potion maker. Not for his football team."

"It's basketball. I don't play football."

"Whatever." Magda folded her arms across her chest.

"I am so screwed." Evan rubbed the back of his neck. "I don't know what to do now."

Magda glanced across the store toward Rachel. She raised her hand, signaling to the other clerk, pointing to the back room where she had taken Evan and Evangeline a few days ago.

The clerk smiled and nodded. She said something to Rachel and pointed to a glass cabinet behind her.

"Diana is going to keep your friend busy. Come with me." Magda turned on her heels and headed toward the short hallway leading to the ingredients room. Evan stood dumbfounded. She was going to help him.

"Well, don't just stand there with your mouth open." Magda stopped and looked over her shoulder.

"Yes ma'am," Evan said, putting his feet into gear.

* * *

EVAN WATCHED AS MAGDA GATHERED DIFFERENT ingredients from mason jars and amber-colored bottles.

"Come here." She tapped the table and motioned for him to join her. Evan cautiously drew up next to her. "First things first. I need your spell book."

"Oh-kay." Evan dug through his backpack until he found the book and handed it to her. "I've got a book-mark on the page."

Magda gave the book a cursory glance before she opened the drawer next to her and tossed the book inside. She closed the drawer quickly and waved her fingers in front of a small lock until it clicked.

"Hey! That's my book." He glared at her.

"Once you've learned a few things, I'll give it back to you. Until then, it stays put."

"But—" Evan protested.

"No buts. Take it up with your aunt if you want it back. For now, it stays put." Magda gave him a pointed look.

Evan rolled his eyes. "Fine. Fine. I don't know how we're going to win now," Evan grumbled.

"If you'll ditch the attitude young man, I will show you how." Magda pointed to the array of things she'd laid out on the table.

"What is all this stuff?"

"This is how you, and only you, will be lucky on the

day of your big-game. Hand me that bag with the Tonka beans and Rue powder that I sold you the other day."

Evan did as he was told. He watched with curiosity as Magda retrieved a small linen bag and a small jelly jar from one of the lower shelves of her table. She opened the paper bag holding Evan's ingredients and up-ended it. Two small plastic bags landed on the table.

"What were you going to do with these?" Magda asked.

Evan shrugged his shoulders. "Whatever the potion told me to do."

"No. No. No," Magda said. "You never just throw ingredients into a pot and call it good. You have to understand how the ingredients work together, or in this case, don't work together. Putting these two things together in a potion, without understanding the proper preparation, is dangerous. The beans have to be carefully sliced in two, boiled until they're soft, then mashed before you ever add the Rue to them."

"That sounds like what Cora does when she cooks our meals," Evan said.

"In some ways it is," Magda said. "Listen, I think for your purposes, the best thing for you is a mojo bag and some blessed oil. Those are the safest options."

"Yes, but will they help me win?"

"Honestly, hon, that really depends on you as much as it does the magic you want to use." Magda cupped his chin and looked deep into his eyes. "You will get out of it what you put into it. If you keep thinking it might not work, it won't work. Do you understand?"

"I guess so," Evan said.

"All right, I'll take that answer," Magda said. "Since it's your mojo bag, you're going to help me build it. It will work better that way."

Evan straightened up. "Great. What do I need to do?"

"First, let's put on some gloves. That Rue can irritate your skin if it's not handled properly."

Alarm bells went off in Evan's head. "What would happen if I put it in a potion and drank it?"

"Oh, honey, it could definitely upset your stomach enough to make you miss that game of yours." Magda winked. "If you know what I mean."

Evan wrinkled his nose in disgust. "Yeah, I think I do know what you mean."

"Good, I'm glad you do. Now, let's get started."

CHAPTER 17

J ason flashed his badge to the young woman behind the security desk. Her dark brown eyes widened, and she pushed her shoulder-length, shaggy hair behind one ear.

"What can I help you with, officer?" She looked young, too young to be sporting gray hair, but the dark pink ends told Jason that she had picked the silvery color on purpose.

"I'm helping out with a case upstairs, and I need to talk to someone in your security division about pulling some video footage for us."

"Okay, I can do that." Her expression a little fearful. "Just give me one minute." She picked up the phone on the desk and dialed. "Hi, it's Gemma at the front desk. I have a police officer here asking to speak to someone about video footage?"

"I'm helping Ben Sutton if that makes a difference," Jason said.

"Did you hear that? Yeah. Okay. I'll let him know," Gemma said, and hung up the phone. "Someone from security's going to come down."

"Great, thank you." Jason gave her his best smile. "I like your hair."

She grinned and dragged her fingers through it down to the pink tips. "Thanks."

From the corner of his eye, Jason caught Tom's expression of disgust and the rolling of his eyes.

"What's your problem?" Jason said, keeping his voice low.

"Nothing," Tom said.

The elevator opened, and a man Jason recognized stepped out. He wore a pair of khaki pants and a black polo shirt with the letters DOL embroidered over the left breast. The snow-colored hair at his temples looked the same, but the silvery mustache he wore was new.

"Gerald, right?" Jason said. He reached out to shake the head of security's hand.

"Yes, sir, it is. I remember you. You're that deputy," Gerald said. He turned and took Tom's hand and gave it a good shake. "And you're a friend of Miss Payne's."

"That's right."

"It's a real shame what's happened her," Gerald said.

"Yes, it is," Jason said. "I was hoping that you could help me out with a couple of things. I've been working with Ben Sutton on finding a way to help Miss Payne."

"Sure. He said something about that. You wanted to look at some security footage."

"Yes, I do. Specifically, the footage in front of Lauren Coldwater's office if possible."

"Yes. She was attacked."

"She was," Jason nodded. "And I'd like to help find who attacked her."

A strange smile spread across Gerald's face causing dark shadows in the creases around his mouth. Jason noticed the bags under the man's eyes for the first time.

"I'm already on top of that," Gerald said.

"You are?" Jason asked. "Mind if I take a look? Also, is there any way to know when people leave the building? I know they have to swipe the badge to go up and then again to get on the elevator but—"

Gerald's grin grew wider. "No. I can't say there is. We know when people get here, but that's about it."

"Right," Jason said. "Well, it was worth a shot. Now, can I take a look at that footage?"

"You know, I've already done that, and I saw no unusual activity outside Ms. Coldwater's office," Gerald said.

"All right, then," Jason said. His internal sensors

pinged. Maybe he'd just been around Lisa and Charlie and the others too long, and maybe there was nothing to it. But everything inside him told him that Gerald was lying. The question was why. What did he have to gain by lying? "Well, we appreciate your time."

"No problem. Are you gonna head back up to Ben's office?" Gerald asked.

"Yeah, we are. Just want to let him know what we found," Jason said.

"Good. Y'all have a good day then," Gerald said. He turned on his heels, swiped his badge, and the elevator opened. Jason kept a smile on his face until the elevator doors closed.

"Great," Tom said. "Now what do we do?"

"Now we go tell Ben."

"Tell him what exactly?" Tom asked.

"Tell him that we have our first suspect. Come on," Jason said.

CHAPTER 18

"What do you mean you think Gerald is a suspect?" Ben asked. The back of his head felt like a woman with very long nails had dug into his scalp and squeezed until sharp pricks of pain penetrated his skull.

First, Jason described his interaction with the security chief, and then laid out his suspicions carefully and methodically. Ben listened, concentrating on the story until finally, Jason stopped talking and gave Ben an expectant look.

"Well?" Jason asked. "What you think?"

Ben rubbed the back of his neck, massaging the tight muscles at the base of the skull. "I think if Gerald said there was nothing on the tape, there's nothing on the tape."

"You don't even want to confirm that?" Jason asked. "Because my spidey-senses were tingling."

"You've been hanging around Charlie too long," Ben said

"Maybe so. And I'd like to keep hanging around her. Wouldn't you?" Jason asked.

"Of course." Ben sighed and opened his desk drawer. He pulled out a small bottle of aspirin, popped the top, and shook three into his hand. He swallowed them with a sip of water and rested his head against the back of his chair. While he waited for the medicine to start working, he closed his eyes for a moment and thought over what Jason had said. He didn't know enough about the security systems in this place, but he knew people who did. His eyes flew open. He sat up, grabbed the handset of his phone, and quickly dialed three digits.

"Hey, Athena," Ben said. "Can you come up here, please?"

A few minutes later, Athena knocked on his door and popped her head into his office. "You wanted to see me?"

"Hey, you work the security desk sometimes, right?" Ben asked.

"I sure do. In fact, I'm technically still on their payroll, not yours." She made an amused face.

"What can you tell me about the badges that we use?" Ben asked.

Athena's gaze shifted from Ben to Jason and Tom.

"It's okay. You can talk in front of them."

"Okay." Athena sat on the corner of Ben's desk. "Here's how it works. Everyone is given a badge when they enter the building, whether it is an official badge like mine and yours, Ben, or a visitor badge like theirs. The chip inside allows you to move throughout the building based on security clearances."

"Does it track when someone comes in and leaves the building?" Ben asked.

"Oh, yeah. It tracks everything. You can see a person's movement once they swipe it the first time and go up the elevator. And then you can see every single time they swipe that badge," Athena said.

"Yeah, but we don't swipe the badge to enter or exit the building," Ben said.

"No, we don't, but the RFID chip pings the database with the timestamp anytime someone walks outside the building. It also pings anytime someone enters the building. That's what keeps up with a person's movements throughout the building."

"See, I told you," Jason said, sounding a little too triumphant.

"Is all this information stored somewhere?" Ben asked.

"Oh, yeah, sure thing. There's not only a database but a backup of the database," Athena said.

"Can you access that database from here?" Ben asked.

"Of course," Athena said. "I just need access to a computer on the network."

Ben stood up and gestured to his chair. Athena sat down, and her fingers began to move deftly over the keyboard.

Jason leaned over and smiled. "Any chance you can access the security camera footage remotely, too?"

Athena glanced up, her green eyes full of light. "You bet."

* * *

THEY ALL STARED IN SILENCE AT THE SCREEN, WATCHING the footage outside Lauren's door. Jason had watched his fair share of video footage, most of it boring him out of his mind. But he also knew when something was wrong.

"Athena, can you play that back for just a second?" Jason asked.

"Sure thing," Athena said. She quickly rewound the digital file. If he hadn't been looking for it the second time through, it would have been easy to miss. Just tiny blip. A jump.

"Is this video time-stamped?" Jason asked.

"I don't know what you're saying, Jason. Can you share what's going on in your head?" Ben asked.

"It's just this really tiny little jump in the footage. Maybe it's been edited," Jason said.

"Wow," Athena said. "You're good. Thirty seconds are missing." Athena pointed to a timeline just below the video footage. "See how it goes from 13:52:26 and it jumps to 13:52:56 here?"

"Can you fast-forward this about five minutes?" Jason asked.

"Of course," Athena said. She gave him a sly smile. "I think I know what you're looking for."

"What is he looking for?" Tom asked.

"I want to see how smart our suspect is," Jason said.

"This still doesn't prove Gerald did it," Ben said.

"Hey, Athena can you tell when this might've been edited?" Jason asked.

"Yeah, there should be a log," Athena said. "I just have to pull up that file." She drew her finger around the touchpad on Ben's laptop until she found exactly what she was looking for and tapped the touchpad twice. The log opened.

"The last person to access this file besides me is username BGHANDLEY." Athena chewed her bottom lip.

"Who is that?" Jason asked.

Ben stared down at the screen. He tightened his arms across his chest.

"It's Gerald Handley," Athena said quietly. She directed her attention to Ben. "What do we do?"

"We..." Ben shook his head. "We proceed with caution.

We need to trap him in the building. Get him to a casting circle and question him."

"You mean question the demon inside him," Jason said.

"We have no proof that he's possessed by a demon," Ben said.

"There was demon dust in Lauren's office," Tom said.

"I know but... I've known Gerald a long time. Since I was a kid. I can't believe—"

"It's not Gerald, though," Tom said. "Not if he's possessed. It's not Gerald."

"I don't know about that," Jason said. All eyes focused on him, and he squirmed in his seat.

"Why do you say that?" Athena asked.

"Because he left Lauren alive. Gerald may still be in there somewhere fighting against this demon. Trying to stop it from wreaking complete havoc," Tom said.

"Why haven't the sensors gone off?" Athena asked.

"Maybe they have," Ben said. "Gerald has obviously doctored security footage. What else has he changed? Not as himself, but as this demon."

"The cleansing herbs have been a little heavy in the past week," Athena said.

"Right, and that's automatic. No one would think twice about it, either. They're so used to it," Ben said.

"Yep," Athena said. She puckered out her bottom lip. "I'm going to ask again, sir. What do we do about it?"

"Let's quietly put together a security team to take him into custody," Ben said. "Athena, I need you to gather your best and most discreet security officers together for this. If there is actually a demon possessing him, then I want us to take extreme care with Gerald. I'm not about to let a forty-year veteran at this company lose his good name because of something happening to him that is out of his control."

"Yes, sir," Athena said. She turned back to the computer and began typing again. "I'm just going to check his whereabouts in the building." Her fingers moved over the touchpad in a graceful rhythm and stopped. "Um, we have a problem."

"What?" Ben and Jason asked in unison. They exchanged a concerned glance.

"According to this log, Gerald Handley left the building twenty-two minutes ago," Athena said.

CHAPTER 19

Ben gathered the others into the conference room. Jen, Lisa, Daphne, and Evangeline sat around the conference table with Tomeka and Darius. Athena, Marigold, and Sabine stood along one wall, with Jason, Tom, Joy, and the reaper Gabrielle standing along the opposite wall.

A murmur of disagreement traveled throughout the room, and Ben held up his hands, trying to quell the crowd.

"Why are we going to Gerald's house," Tom protested. "He could be out of the city by now, on his way to the West Coast for all we know. We need to concentrate on finding Gabrielle's book."

"I agree," Ben said. "Let's just think about this logically, okay? He attacked Lauren in her office and took the book with him."

"You think," Tom said. "Even you said there's no proof he took it."

"I know," Ben said. "But if he left the building, and he had the book with him —"

"A big if," Tom said.

"Then, we will be better off just going to his house and confronting him. The worst thing that could happen is the book's not there," Ben said.

"I'm all for going to this human's house if it means I can retrieve my book," Gabrielle said. The haughtiness of her manner and the sharp angles of Gabrielle's face and body reminded Ben of one of those skeletal models in the fashion magazines that Jen sometimes read. Her black turtleneck, black pants, and harsh make-up job didn't help to soften her image. If he didn't know already that she was a reaper, he would have suspected it, just from the way she presented herself.

"We don't have time for a wild goose chase," Tom said. "We need to... We need to find that book as soon as possible. Surely there must be another way." Tom glanced at Lisa and Jen down at the end of the table with an imploring expression on his face.

Lisa shifted in her chair and rested her hands on the table in front of her. "I think I may have an idea about how to do that."

"Please," Ben said. "I'm open to ideas at this point."

"I noticed you have a ring on your finger, Gabrielle," Lisa said, pointing toward the reaper's hand. Gabrielle lifted the hand with the ring and cradled it against her chest.

"Yes," Gabrielle said.

"I think we can use your ring to find your book," Lisa said. She laced her fingers together and met Ben's eyes. "A location spell should do it. That way we can find the book in time. Then you can send a team to get the book, and another team to retrieve Gerald, and everybody's happy."

Ben rocked on his feet and thought over her proposition. Finally, he nodded. "Okay. It shouldn't take too long to set something up."

"Great," Lisa said.

"What do you need?" Ben asked.

"A casting circle, some crystals, some candles, Gabrielle's ring, and some maps," Lisa said.

Ben turned his attention to Athena. "Can you help Lisa with that?"

Athena sat up straight in her chair, her curls bouncing a little when she nodded. "You bet."

* * *

BEN LED THEM TO THE FOURTH-FLOOR CASTING ROOM. HE slipped in next to Jen and said, "I wish we were doing this under better circumstances. I always intended to bring you here sometime."

The elevator opened and interrupted him. He had looked forward to the expression on Jen's face when she first saw the setup. Now she just looked tired and worried, and the guilt he felt about her worry gnawed at his gut.

"This place is amazing," Daphne said, and slipped off her shoes. She stepped onto the green grassy floor and rocked back and forth.

"It certainly is," Jen said, moving closer to Ben. She leaned against his arm. "I can see why Charlie likes it here so much."

"And she will like it again," Tom said, sidling up next to her. "If it's the last thing I do."

"Don't say things like that, Tom. It would kill Charlie if she gained her life and you lost yours," Jen scolded.

"Jen's right," Ben said. Athena bounded through an open door carrying what looked like a rolled-up map in one hand.

"I found it," Athena said, holding up the map. "It's the largest one we have."

"Great," Lisa said. She unfurled the corner of the map and appeared to give it a cursory scan. "I'll take that if you don't mind. Where's the best place to set up?"

"Athena, can you show Lisa the center of the casting circle?" Ben asked.

"Of course," Athena said. "I also checked on that other

thing we talked about."

"And?" Ben asked.

"I looked up Gerald's address and put it into the maps app on my phone. Once we're done here, we'll be ready to start searching for him at ground zero," Athena said.

"Ground zero?" Ben asked.

Athena shrugged. "That's what I'm calling his house."

"Good. I think we're prepared for any scenario then," Ben said.

Athena nodded. "Come on, Lisa. I'll show you where you can set up."

LISA HAD ASKED FOR BLACK CANDLES AND INSISTED THAT everyone step inside the stones that made up the casting circle. On a table in the center of the casting circle, Lisa spread the map. The energy in the room thrummed, becoming palpable. Lisa gave a nod to her aunt, and Evangeline lit her candle, then used the flame to light Jen's. When her candle flared, Jen lit the next candle, and so it went until all the candles burned. Lisa carefully retrieved Gabrielle's reaper ring from her front pocket and carefully threaded a long piece of red string through it before tying it into a loop.

She moved closer to the table and looked down at the map of the United States in front of her.

"I'm going to do this by geographical region," Lisa announced. "Starting in the South. If this proves successful, we may need more maps."

"Don't worry," Athena said. "We have plenty of maps."

"Let's begin." Lisa gave her a nod and closed her eyes. She thrust her hand out over the map. She opened her fingers, holding tight to the red string and let the ring fall.

"Blessed Goddess, hear my prayer," Lisa said. The witches around her softly echoed her words.

"Thank you for granting my desire," Lisa said. She imagined a light, warm and bright, glowing inside her chest while she spoke the incantation.

"What was stolen shall now be found. Where ere it be, the whole world around."

The ring began to move in a small circle at first. Then, it grew larger and larger still. Lisa continued to chant, her words reiterated by the witches standing around her. The ring spun and tugged against the thread. The words *Find the Reaper's Book* popped into her head, and she found her lips uttering them instead of her incantation. The witches followed her lead, changing their chant. Her heart pounded against her ribs, and a small voice inside her head screamed, "You're doing it wrong."

But no matter how hard she tried, she couldn't seem to go back to her incantation. Lisa pushed the voice down deep until she could barely hear it. The ring spun harder until the thread popped, sending it into the air.

Lisa's eyes flew open, and she watched as the ring flew up and out before landing on its edge. The witches moved in closer to the table and watched the ring circle the entire map of the United States, Canada, and Mexico. It rolled with purpose.

"Find the reaper's book," Lisa whispered at first. Then she repeated it louder. Daphne joined in. Then Jen. And Evangeline. Soon the others chanted along with her. The ring sailed across Alabama, before taking a sharp left at the Florida Panhandle. It traveled along the Appalachian Trail before turning again toward Charlotte. It circled the large city on the map as if it were looking for its destination.

Lisa watched the ring spiral away from the city before it finally stopped and fell down on its side. A collective gasp traveled through the witches around her. Lisa stopped chanting and peered through the ring down at the map.

"How far is Lake Norman from here?" Lisa asked.

"About an hour depending on traffic," Ben said.

"That's where we're going to find it," Lisa said.

"Lake Norman's a big place," Ben said.

Lisa nodded. "You're right. We're gonna need another map to narrow it down."

"Athena pulled her phone from her back pocket and held it up for the others to see. "I already have a map that will work. Gerald Handley's house is on Lake Norman."

CHAPTER 20

"Lisa, you, Jen, and Evangeline are with me," Ben said.

"What about me?" Jason asked.

"I appreciate that you want to be there, but I figured you would probably want to stay here with Charlie. I mean, this is a little out of your depth really," Ben said.

"I am going to disagree with you on that. I think you need as many people as possible, witch or not," Jason argued. "And if there's anything I know how to do, it's how to apprehend a suspect."

"A possessed suspect? I don't know, that demon's going to give Gerald super-human strength," Ben said.

"That's all right. I've got something in my trunk that might temper that super-human strength."

"What exactly?" Ben asked.

"A stun gun,"

"A stun gun," Ben said, his tone doubtful.

"Yep. Even if it doesn't bring him down, it could slow him up enough for y'all to do that thing you do with your wands," Jason said.

Ben scrubbed his chin. "Fine. You can come. Just make sure you don't stun anyone other than Gerald."

"No problem," Jason said.

"Ben, do you mind if I stay behind?" Tomeka asked. "I'd like to continue sitting with Charlie, if that's okay. Darius would too. Wouldn't you, Darius?"

A look of surprise widened Darius's eyes, and his brows rose halfway up his forehead. "Sure. I'd be happy to stay here with Charlie and you. If Daphne doesn't mind."

Daphne slipped her hand into Darius's and gave it a squeeze. "I don't mind at all. In fact, it would make me feel better if y'all were with her."

"I agree with Daphne," Lisa said.

"Oh, Goddess, somebody please record that for posterity's sake," Daphne joked. Jen and Evangeline chuckled, but Lisa didn't seem to find it funny.

Ben cocked his head and considered Tomeka's request. What was Tomeka up to? He didn't want to embarrass her. She'd really become part of the team in just the few days she'd been working at the DOL, volunteering to do whatever was needed to help with Charlie's case.

"All right. You two stay here. Let us know if there's any change," Ben said.

"Absolutely," Tomeka said. "Y'all be careful. Come on, Darius." She pinched his sleeve and led him away from the group.

"Y'all be careful." Darius pecked Daphne on the lips before being dragged away by his sister. "Text me if you need me."

Ben watched the two of them disappear from the room before turning his attention back to his crew. "All right. Tom, are you, Joy, and Gabrielle going to meet us there?"

"Yes," Tom said.

"Great. Athena, do you still have skills with that blow gun of yours?"

"I do," she nodded.

"Good. Get it, along with the strongest sedative you find, then gather the others and come in a separate car."

"Yes, sir," Athena said.

"Where do you want me, boss?" Will asked.

Ben scratched his head. "I... I don't know. How familiar are you with hunting demons?"

"They're not really different than vamps. They have their own smell, and they leave that damn dust every-where. And as far as dispatching them, I've got a knife for that."

"A knife that will kill demons?" Jason asked. "Where did you get one?"

"This one was forged in the bowels of hell. I paid a pretty price for it on the black market. But you didn't hear that from me," Will said.

"And it works?" Jason asked.

"Like a charm," Will said.

"Yeah, I'm just going to ignore that last part," Ben said. "I have no plans to kill Gerald. If he's still alive somewhere inside that body of his, I'd like to just exorcise the damn demon and, maybe if we're lucky, save Gerald's life."

"If you can get the demon out of the host body," Tom said, "we can ensure the demon goes back to where he belongs. It will be tricky, and the timing will have to be perfect. We'll have to drop our glamours to do it, but no one has to die if we can help it."

"Good. That's exactly the way I want it," Ben said.

"Sounds like a plan," Will said, rubbing his hands together. "Let's go demon hunting."

CHAPTER 21

Tomeka pulled one of the padded stools up next to Charlie's bedside. Her lips had turned blue, and her pale blonde hair lay limp off her face, wet and stringy in places. Tomeka wrapped her hand around Charlie's forearm. The cold, clammy skin made her stomach turn. She focused her gaze on the monitors and the slow beep of Charlie's heartbeat.

"Hey, Charlie," Tomeka said. "It's me, Mika. I don't know if you can hear me or not. Darius is here with me. Although he stopped to get some coffee."

Tomeka reached inside her bag and pulled out her deck of tarot cards.

"I know this is crazy. I rely on these cards way too much. And I don't even know if they will bridge the gap between here and wherever you are."

Darius pushed open the door carrying two cups of fresh coffee in his hands. Tomeka took one of the cups and took a sip, glad for the warmth in this cold, cold place.

"I'm here, Mika," Darius said. "Now you gonna tell me why you really didn't want to go with them?"

"I thought since you're a necromancer, your talents would be better used here with Charlie. Maybe you can call her up and let her know that we're fighting for her life. That we're doing everything we can."

"I would love to talk to her," Darius said. "Just one problem. Charlie's not really dead."

"What do you mean? She's almost dead," Tomeka said.

"I know, but she's not all the way dead. I know she's not here. I can see there's nobody home. But she's not there, either. She's somewhere in between." Darius shook his head. "All we can do now is just stay here and be with her. Hopefully, our energy will anchor hers to this plane, at least while this body is still alive."

Tomeka twirled one of her braids around her finger and leaned with her elbows on the table next to where Charlie lay so cold and still. She shuffled her deck of cards and cut it in half. Then she brought the two halves back together and pressed the deck into Charlie's palm. She drew the first card. And a smile tugged at her lips.

"This is you, Charlie," Tomeka said. She positioned

the high priestess card on Charlie's flat stomach. "She represents knowledge and understanding and intuition and dreams. I couldn't have picked a better card myself."

When Tomeka drew the next card, her heart beat a little faster.

"The moon. My guess is that you might be a little confused right now, maybe even a little overwhelmed. A little fearful of what you're going through and what might happen in the future. But the other thing this card tells me about you is that you need to trust yourself. Don't be afraid. Even if you're surrounded by darkness at this moment. You're not alone."

"Keep talking to her, Mika. Keep talking." Darius put his hand on his sister's shoulder and gave it a gentle squeeze. "Maybe your voice will be enough to keep her grounded."

Tomeka nodded, took a deep breath, and drew another card.

Tears stung her eyes, and she put the five of cups down next to the moon card.

"I don't want you to be scared, but this is not the card I really wanted to see. You need to hang on. You hear me, Charlie Payne? You can change your future. You don't have to be afraid of it."

"Keep talking, Mika. Don't stop," Darius said.

Tomeka took the cards away from Charlie's chest and folded the three drawn cards into the deck. She slipped the deck back into her purse and took Charlie's frozen hand into her own.

"I'm here, Charlie."

THE LIGHT BEHIND HER GREW BRIGHTER AND WARMER. Charlie was almost certain that, even though she had not moved from her spot, the light had moved closer to her. All she wanted to do was turn around and let it embrace her for good. To be done with this fight.

The feel of someone holding her hand made her look down to see where it came from. There did not seem be to anyone here with her, but in the distance, she heard voices. Voices she knew well. Voices telling her to hang on.

And for a moment she held on, but that light, it beckoned to her, vibrated around her and through her.

How could she not want to be part of it? Finally, when she could stand it no more, she turned to face it, and in the blink of an eye, it swallowed her whole.

THE RHYTHMIC SOUND OF WAVES CRASHING AGAINST THE beach made Charlie open her eyes. She found herself standing on a familiar beach, although she couldn't quite place it. The shore seemed to extend forever in both directions, and fat, white puffy clouds floated in the distance. The sun sat low in the sky, and the day was warm, but not hot, and strangely not humid.

She looked down to find herself in a pair of white linen shorts and a long-sleeved, white linen blouse over a pale blue tank top. Her toes dug into the sand, and she relished the warmth.

Charlie took a seat on the sand and watched the sun sink lower in the sky, turning the clouds from white to pale pink and deep orange.

"Charlie, girl?" a familiar voice called after her.

Charlie looked up the beach and saw her grandmother approaching. She wore a pink plaid blouse over a white tank top and a pair of khaki Capri pants. Her silvery-white hair glowed in the light of the sunset. Bunny waved, and a big smile crossed her face.

"Hey, Bunny." Charlie waved back. "Come watch the sunset with me."

Charlie blinked, and the next thing she knew her grandmother was beside her.

"We weren't expecting you," Bunny said.

"I know. I just couldn't seem to stay away. I tried. I tried so hard."

"I know, love. I know. There's still time for you to go back."

A loud, beeping sound penetrated Charlie's

consciousness. The frantic sounds of voices filled her head.

Charlie looked up, searching for the sound. "Do you hear that?"

"Hear what, love?"

"It sounds like heartbeats or something mechanical beeping." Charlie stood up, still searching for the source.

"Oh, that," Bunny said. "That's just the doctors. They are probably trying to save your life. You may have gone into cardiac arrest. That would be my guess, anyway. Why don't you come sit down, sweetie? This is going to be one doozy of a sunset." Bunny tapped the sand next to her.

"What am I doing here? I should not be here." Panic fluttered in Charlie's chest, and she began to walk away from her grandmother. Within a few seconds, her grandmother stood in front of her.

"Now, just wait a minute. At the moment, you don't have anywhere to go back to. Be still and listen." Bunny pointed to the sky. Charlie followed her grandmother's finger. Looking upward, she could see the universe. Stars glowed against the deep black sky. Planets. Nebulas.

"Bunny?" Charlie called. Panic wound its way through her chest. "Bunny!?"

"WHAT'S HAPPENING TO HER?" TOMEKA CRIED. DARIUS

held her back from the table.

"She's stable for now. She had a seizure," the doctor said. "Do you know where her family is?"

"They're off looking for something that will cure her," Tomeka said.

"Right. This was Sutton's idea." The doctor sighed and scrubbed his fingers through his short brown hair. "I hope whatever it is they're doing, they get here quick. I don't know how much longer we can keep her in this state. She's already starting to deteriorate. If she has another seizure, we could lose her."

"Okay, doctor, thank you," Tomeka said. She pulled her phone from her purse and jotted off a text to Ben.

Charlie going downhill fast. Have you found the book?

Tomeka stared at the screen, but no answer came. She jotted off a text to Jen, letting her know the situation. It took less than a second for three dots to appear with a response from Jen.

Please tell her to hang on. And you need to let her ex, Scott know. So he can tell her son. Maybe Scott can bring him to Charlotte.

Is that a good idea? He's kind of young, isn't he?

I know it's hard, but yes he should be told. I'll tell you the story about my mom's death sometime. We were kept away. It was awful. Tell Scott to bring Evan.

Okay. Do you have his number?

Yes. I'll look it up and text it to you.

CHAPTER 22

I t took almost an hour to get to Lake Norman with late afternoon traffic working against them.

Jason circled the block to get a good look at the layout of the house and the surrounding land. In a community of older two-story homes built in the seventies, Gerald's yellow clapboard house sat back from the street near the water, on a large, mostly wooded lot. With white shutters and a formal portico, the house seemed to be built into the hill leading down to the lake.

A separate, matching two-car garage sat adjacent to the house, and when Jason slowed down to check as much of the back of the house as he could from the street, he saw a boat shelter near a short dock extending into the lake. It would be a lot to search. Maybe once this thing was contained, Ben could call for more reinforcements to help.

When he felt like he knew what they were in for, he parked down the street. He popped the trunk and got out. This wasn't his case, wasn't even his jurisdiction, but he damn sure wasn't going in there unarmed. His hand hovered over the lockbox holding his weapon and he kept it moving to another box that held a taser and a stun gun. He took both and held them in his hand to weigh them out before finally settling on the stun gun. He grabbed his Kevlar vest, more out of habit than anything else, and closed the trunk.

"Do you really think that will drop a demon?" Lisa sidled up next to him.

"I don't know. We'll find out." He leaned over and kissed her on the cheek. "It'll all be fine. Do you think you could say a quick blessing over them?"

"Of course," she said. She placed one hand on each item and whispered a quick prayer to the goddess. When she was done she took a deep breath and gave him a weary smile. "There. Your talismans are blessed. You should be good to go. Just... Just be careful, okay?"

"Back atcha, babe," he said. He thought she might pick a fight. Sometimes she did when she was scared, but instead, she leaned over, pressed her hand against his chest and gave him a quick kiss. Her lips whispered against his for a second before she pulled away.

"What was that for?"

"Just a little extra protection for that body I love so much," she said. "Now be careful."

"I will," he said, and quickly donned his vest.

"Good." She gave him a quick nod. "Let's go round up this demon."

"You got it," he said, answering the determination in her voice with a dark glance at the house.

They made their way up to the end of the driveway and waited for Ben, Jen, Daphne, and Will to get out of Ben's FJ50. Athena and the other witches had parked up the street out of sight and joined them a few minutes later. Jason's belly began to tingle like it did anytime he took part in a S.W.A.T operation.

"Okay," Ben said. "Evangeline, if you wouldn't mind setting up a protection circle around the house with the help of Daphne, Lisa, and Jen, that would be great."

"You don't want our help? You know, taking him down?" Jen asked.

"This will be a big help. We need to protect Gerald's neighbors in case Tom and his crew can't catch this demon."

"Do not worry yourself, witch," Gabrielle said. "We will not allow the demon to get away."

"Evangeline is powerful enough to cast that spell without us," Lisa said. "Jen, Daphne, and I all have experience with casting out demons, as you well know."

"I do know," Ben said. "I also know how dangerous the last time was, and I don't want anyone to get hurt or possessed unnecessarily."

"No one is going to possess me, Daphne, or Jen." Lisa swept her hair aside to show a tiny tattoo at the base of her hair line behind one of her ears — a pentacle between two crescent moons.

Jen removed the old Timex watch she wore and held her wrist up to show her matching tattoo.

"What about you?" Ben asked, directing his question to Daphne.

Her eyes widened, and she glanced around the group.

"Oh, um, mine is somewhere a little more private," she said. "But it's there."

"We got them after our last demon encounter, just to be on the safe side," Jen said.

Ben lowered his voice and bent over. "I thought you said you hurt yourself at work."

Jen shrugged. "I lied. I'm sorry. I just know how much you hate tattoos. I didn't want you to try and talk me out of it. Are you mad?"

"No. Not really. I just don't know how I didn't catch the lie?" Ben said.

Jen smiled and pecked him on the cheek. "There may have been some misdirection on my part."

"You sneaky little witch," Ben said, grinning.

"So, does Charlie have one too?" Jason asked.

"Yes," Jen and Tom said at the same time, then chuckled.

"I can verify that she does. It's also in a discreet place." Tom pasted a self-satisfied grin on his face before he went serious again.

"So, Jen and I will go with Tom, Gabrielle, and Joy," Lisa said.

"For the record, I don't like this. I'd feel better if you stayed here with Evangeline," Jason said.

"Nice try, deputy, but not happening," Lisa said.

"Wait. Evangeline, will you please help me out here?" Jason said.

"Sorry, honey," Evangeline said. "And the fact that they're going with Tom is actually better."

"Better how? It's not like they're armed," Jason said.

"Don't worry about us, lieutenant," Joy practically purred. "We're armed. You just can't see it."

"And trust me, you don't want to," Lisa said, giving Joy a side-eyed look. "No offense."

"None taken," Joy said.

"Shall we go now?"

"Yes," Ben said. "Jason, you, Athena, Marigold, and Sabine take the front door. Will and I will flank the house from the left. Tom, you lead your group around the right."

Tom nodded. "I'll let you know if we spot him in any of the windows."

"How are you gonna do that? We don't have any radios?" Jason said.

Tom stared at him, a smug look on his face.

Like this lieutenant.

Jason scowled. "What the fuck? You can get inside my head?"

I can't read your thoughts if that's what you're asking. Unless you decide to communicate with me mentally.

"The last thing I want to do is communicate with you mentally," Jason said.

"You can communicate with me." Ben looked around. "And Athena."

"Cool," Athena chirped with a little more enthusiasm than Jason thought was necessary.

"Very well." Tom cleared his throat. "All any of you have to do, to communicate with me, is think my name. That will open the lines of communication. No need to speak out loud. Do you understand?"

"Yes," Ben said. The others nodded or murmured, "Yes."

"Great. Now that we know how we're talking to each other, we've all got our jobs. Let's get to this."

* * *

EVAN HELD TIGHT TO THE MOJO BAG IN HIS POCKET. THE texture, strangely both rough and soft, felt good against the skin of his thumb, and he stroked it any time Rachel's arm brushed up against his in the back seat of the Uber.

"You sure you don't want to come in and have dinner with us? It will probably just be me and Cora. My dad tends to work late these days," Evan said.

"That's really sweet. I appreciate it. But for once, my mother is actually expecting me home. She said she wanted to go to dinner and tell me something," Rachel said.

The sparkle of the amethyst pendant that now hung around her neck caught his attention. "That's a good stone then to be wearing."

Rachel's hand immediately reached for the pendant. She gave him a quizzical look.

"Amethyst is protective. It's good at warding off negative emotions and forces," he said, with a faint smile.

"Protective," Rachel said, looking deep into his eyes. "I like that. Where did you learn that?"

"My mom. She's big on the crystals. My whole family is actually," Evan said. "My cousin Jen has this huge collection."

"Sounds like something my mom would believe in." Rachel tipped her chin and looked at him from beneath her long lashes. "Evan Carver, you know, you're not like any other boy I've ever known."

His stomach did a somersault. *Keep it cool Ev. Keep it cool.* "That's a good thing, right?"

"It is," she said. The red Jeep Cherokee Uber pulled into his driveway and parked.

Rachel didn't stop staring at him, and it shocked him when she quickly leaned over and pressed her warm lips to his. "See you tomorrow?"

"Um... yeah," *Keep it COOL EV.* "Yeah. See you tomorrow."

Evan got out of the car, his whole body tingling and numb at the same time. He stood on the porch and watched until the taillights of the Cherokee turned the corner and disappeared. The mojo bag was already working.

"We're going to win," he muttered. "We're gonna win!"

He jumped into the air, and his fingers brushed the ceiling of the porch. "We're gonna win!" he yelped again.

"Evan! What are you doing out here, son?" His father's stern voice pulled him out of his reverie for just a second.

Evan grinned and faced his father. "We're gonna win, Dad."

"I'm sure you will. Why don't you come inside? I need to talk to you about something."

"What is it?" All the excitement from his kiss disappeared.

"It's about your mother. Now, come on. Let's eat dinner before it gets cold. Cora has set the table."

"Yes, sir," Evan said. He slung his backpack over his shoulder and headed into the house.

CHAPTER 23

Ben led Will around Gerald's house. They stopped at every window to take a quick peek before ducking down, lower than the windowsill, out of sight.

His heart leaped into his throat when he spied Gerald on the dining room floor leaning against a wall. In one hand, he held a gun; he cradled the other hand against his chest. Ben spotted a large Herkimer crystal on the floor next to his feet. Gerald's dark skin glistened with sweat. Dark, wet circles outlined the underarms and collar of his blue polo shirt. He banged his head against the wall, and enormous turmoil filled every line of his face. Even through the closed window, Ben heard Gerald mumbling, *Get out*, to himself.

Ben flattened himself against the wall outside the

window, and Will did the same. Ben pointed to the window, and Will nodded, indicating he understood, then put his hand beneath the flap of the bag he wore across his body. When he pulled his hand out, he held a large bladed knife. Ben shook his head wildly.

"Last resort," Will mouthed.

Ben's jaw tightened, and he reluctantly nodded his head. He didn't like the idea of having to kill Gerald. It made him sick to his stomach to even entertain such a thought, but, in the end, he faced reality. He might not have another choice.

Ben peeked in the window again. The sight of Gerald sent him reeling backward. No more tears and emotional turmoil. Whatever concern had tormented Gerald moments earlier had evaporated. Now his countenance was a study in black irises and haughtiness as, paralyzed now, Ben stared at the barrel of Gerald's gun pointing at him, freezing him to the spot.

Will peered quickly into the window. He yanked on Ben's arm, tackling his boss. The two of them landed hard and rolled toward the foundation. Two gunshots rang out. Ben waited a beat before pushing his back up against the outer wall and rising to his feet. Will followed his lead.

"Tom," Ben said aloud.

Tom's voice filtered through Ben's head. *We are already on it.* Now he understood Jason's shocked reaction earlier. The feeling of someone else inside his head unnerved him.

"You okay, boss?" Will asked.

"Yeah," Ben said. "As okay as I can be. I've never been shot at before. At least not with a gun."

"Understandable," Will said.

"We need to get in there. Tom and his group are already on the move. Jen —" Ben said.

"Say no more, sir," Will said. The two of them stayed low until they turned the corner. A long, wide deck overlooking the lake rose before them with a patio beneath the deck. A picnic table with benches and an outdoor seating arrangement of a couch and two chairs looked out over the water. Gerald had done well for himself. No wonder he had called this place his haven.

Ben's gut tightened. Across the patio he could see Tom, with Jen and Lisa sandwiched between Joy and Gabrielle. Ben gestured toward the pair of wide French sliders that opened onto the patio. The doors closest to Tom were open. The screen wasn't even closed. What did the demon care if the house filled with mosquitoes and flies? Ben scurried up to the set of doors nearest him and peeked inside. It looked like some sort of game room with a pool table, a long leather couch, and another room off to one side. Ben gestured to Tom to follow him in on three.

Then another shot rang out. Ben went first. Will and

Tom followed closely on his heels. Ben could hear movement over their heads. He pointed to the ceiling and held his wand in a defensive position in case Gerald surprised them. Although his wand would not stop a bullet, maybe he could slow it down. The three of them cautiously approached the stairs to the main level of the house.

"Does anyone know if Gerald is married?" Jen whispered.

"He's divorced," Ben said. "What does it matter?"

He stopped on the top step. The basement door was closed tight. Ben jiggled the handle and found it locked. Not that he'd ever come across a lock that could stop him. He whispered a quick unlocking spell and heard the mechanism turn.

"I'm just wondering if there are other people to consider upstairs," Jen said. "We need to be careful."

"Jen's right," Lisa said. "We don't need any casualties today if we can help it.."

"Except, of course a demon," Gabrielle said. "I will happily accept his death."

"I didn't think demons really died," Will said.

"Did you not boast that the knife in your hands is a demon killer?" Gabrielle asked.

"It is. But honestly, I just assumed it sent them back to hell," Will said.

"If y'all are done with philosophizing about demons, and where they go, I've got the door unlocked," Ben said.

As quietly as he could, he turned the knob and pushed the door open. Three more shots rang out.

"That's six," Will said.

"So?" Lisa said.

"He had a revolver. He's out of bullets," Will said.

"Unless he's got extra ammo on him," Lisa countered.

"Well, we better move fast," Ben said. "Before he can reload."

Ben took a deep breath and stepped into the kitchen.

Once they were all out of the basement, he signaled for them to split up. He grabbed Jen by the wrist. "Why don't you come with me?"

"Lisa may need me," Jen said.

"I need you more," Ben said.

Jen opened her mouth as if to argue.

"It's fine, Jen. Go with him," Lisa said. "Go."

Ben tucked Jen between himself and Will, making sure to stay in front of her as they made their way through the house. The sound of a struggle and furniture being knocked around made Ben speed up. They rounded the corner and rushed past the stairway into the living room. Jason and Gerald were on the floor, fighting over the gun in Gerald's hand.

"Athena!" Ben said. She stood on the sidelines, seemingly hypnotized by the sight of them struggling, her right arm bleeding.

"Athena, move." Ben pointed his wand at Gerald and began to chant.

DEMON HEAD, DEMON HEART, I COMMAND YOU.
I cast you out of this body. Leave this realm. Go home.
To the netherworld, where you belong.

JEN, DAPHNE, AND LISA JOINED IN THE CHANT, AND ALL three of their wands emitted streams of pale, yellow light. Ben and Jen worked from one side with Lisa and Daphne on another. The light wrapped around Gerald's body like a lasso and tightened like a vise. Sabine and Marigold raised their wands and joined in. Ben raised his wand higher.

"Do what I do," he commanded the witches.

Lisa, Jen, and the others followed his actions and raised their arms and wands higher into the air.

Gerald's body lifted. He struggled against the light, kicking and screaming, trying to move his arms. Jason rolled out from underneath him. Ben began his chant again.

DEMON HEAD, DEMON HEART, I COMMAND YOU.
I cast you out of this body. Leave this realm. Go home.

To the netherworld, where you belong.

A GROWL DEEP INSIDE GERALD'S CHEST ESCAPED HIS BODY and then he grew quiet. Too quiet. After a few moments, he stopped struggling. The light lasso had pinned his arms but left his hands free. He closed his eyes and tucked his chin under. Then he raised his hands and grabbed two of the streams of light trapping him. He jerked on them as if they were ropes. He yanked Lisa and Jen forward, pulling them off balance. Jen toppled on to her hands and knees. Lisa tripped over the carpet and fell to the ground. Gerald landed on his feet.

Ben shot off a round of hot yellow light and hit Gerald in the side. He turned toward Ben, his face molding into a mask of hate and rage. Gerald's eyes flared, and Ben shot at him again, hitting him squarely in the chest. A buzzing sound filled the air, and Gerald slapped at his neck as if a bug had bitten him. Something small, black, and sharp fell to the floor.

"What the hell was that?" Jen grabbed Ben's hand and he helped her to her feet. He pointed to Athena across the room. She held a small blow gun to her mouth with her good hand. As they raised their wands again, another small black projectile whizzed through the air and hit Gerald in the neck again. Then another hit him in the shoulder. He let out a cry of anger and pain and swiped at the two darts penetrating his skin.

"Why, you little witch," he said. He started toward Athena, but his knees buckled after two steps, and he fell face forward on the ground.

"Is he dead?" Jason asked. He stood up and tapped his toe against Gerald's splayed arms.

"No," Athena said. "He'll wake up with a nasty headache. But he's not dead."

Athena swayed on her feet, and Jason reached out to prop her up. "You've been shot. Jen, she's been shot."

"Let's get her to Evangeline," Jen said. "She can at least stop the bleeding until we can get her back to the medical center."

Tom sidled up next to Ben. "What shall we do with him?"

"Well, that demon still has hold of him. We're gonna have to take him back to the DOL and exorcise the demon," Ben said.

"What about the book?" Tom asked.

"Let's tear this place apart and see if we can find it. We'll bind him up and keep him out cold until we can get him back to the DOL."

"Good idea. Joy, Gabrielle, and I will start on the top floor," Tom said.

"Good. Lisa, Will, and I will take care of this floor and the basement," Ben said. "I'm gonna head back to the

DOL with Evangeline and Athena to make sure she gets the care she needs. You all continue the search."

"Good idea," Tom said. "Just be careful."

"I will. And you text me as soon as you find the book. Charlie's life may depend on it."

"You have my word," Tom said, casting a glance at Gabrielle. She stood near Gerald's body, and looked around before landing a soft kick into his thigh.

CHAPTER 24

J ason ripped through the walk-in closet in the
master bedroom, checking every shelf, knocking
on the wall looking for hollow places. Gerald
had more pairs of khakis than Jason did, and
Jason practically lived in khakis. He threw another pair
on the floor and looked at the bare walls.

"Anything?" Will asked.

"Nothing." Jason stepped outside the closet. He found
Will with one hand propped up against one of the four
posters of the mahogany bed. A bank of windows gave a
breathtaking view of the lake. Just looking at the last of
the day's sun rippling across the water calmed him down.

"I take it you haven't found anything either?"

"No. I've got the two female reapers guarding the pris-
oner for now. The other one, Tom, he decided to head

back to the medical center to be with Charlie." Will turned and appeared to take in the view. "I could get used to this."

"Yeah, me too," Jason said.

"The sedative has worn off, and Gerald's conscious again. I just hope those bindings hold until the transport from the DOL gets here," Will said.

"Lisa, Daphne, and Jen could hold him if necessary. I've seen 'em do it. Although I don't know for how long," Jason said.

"Yeah, that's what Lisa said." Will rubbed the back of his neck and took a seat on the bed. "I knew I'd see some action when I took this job. I just didn't expect it to happen on the first case, and I'm not getting any younger."

"I hear you on that. What did you do before this?" Jason asked.

"I'm a vampire hunter," Will said.

"Are you serious? Or are you just yanking my chain?" Jason asked.

"I'm serious as a heart attack," Will said. "I've hunted a few demons, although I've never taken great care to keep one alive. Usually, once a person is possessed, they're either dead or they go insane. Either way, I don't see a good way out for this Gerald."

"Yeah," Jason said. "That's been my experience, too. Hopefully, though, if we can exorcise it, maybe there something the DOL can do. Some spell. Some psychological intervention."

"Maybe." Will shrugged, but Jason got the feeling he didn't believe in such things. "I'm gonna head down and see if the others need help. You okay up here?"

"Yes, should be," Jason said.

Will started toward the door. The floor creaked loud enough to draw Jason's attention. Why hadn't he noticed that before?

"Stop!" Jason said.

Will froze in his tracks, turned, and gave Jason a curious look. "What's going on?"

"I think there's a loose floorboard," Jason said.

Will bounced up and down and no creak.

"I swear I heard something," Jason said.

Will nodded and stepped off the rug. He knelt on the hardwood floor and rolled up one corner of the expensive Persian rug. Jason knelt next to the opposite corner and flipped it up. The two of them began knocking on the floor, looking for loose boards.

"There's some give in this one." Will dug his fingers into the cracks between boards and was able to lift it up about half an inch.

"The bed is weighing it down. Give me a hand."

Jason jumped to his feet, and, with Will's help, moved the large mahogany fourposter bed over from the center of the wall several inches. Will lifted the floorboard up with ease.

"I see something," he said.

"Let's get it out." Jason moved close to the opening and peered down into the space between the floor joists which was just enough to hide a large book.

"I'm not touching that thing. Charlie told me it was cursed. It could kill us because we're human," Will said.

"How the hell are we supposed to get it out then?" Jason asked.

"It's a reaper's book, and we've got two of them downstairs. I'm guessing they can touch it," Will said.

"Right."

"I'll be right back. Do not touch it. It can get in your head, so you may not want to stand too close to it," Will said.

"Good to know." Jason took a step back.

A few minutes later, Will returned with Joy and Gabrielle.

"Who is guarding the demon guy?" Jason asked.

"The witches," Joy said. "Don't worry. There is no reason to think he could overpower them, from what my brother tells me."

"I have no doubt they could handle it. But I'll still feel better about all of this once you get that book out, and he's transported back to the DOL headquarters," Jason said.

272

"I'll feel better once I have my book and that demon is back where he belongs," Gabrielle said.

Jason held up his hands in surrender. "You'll get no argument from me."

"Where is it?" Gabrielle asked. Jason pointed at the open space in the floor. Gabrielle quickly retrieved her book, hugging it against her chest.

Jason's phone chirped in his pocket, indicating he had a text. He quickly pulled it out and glanced down at the screen. It was from Ben.

Did you find the book? Just got a message from Tomeka. Charlie is getting worse. Need to speed this along. Wake him up if you have to.

Dread tied Jason's stomach into a cold knot.

"Charlie's in trouble. We need to get him out of here."

"We need to do more than that," Gabrielle said. She held the open book in front of her and didn't seem to bother to contain her ire. "This is not my book."

"Are you sure?" Jason asked.

"Absolutely. This is just some family grimoire," Gabrielle complained, and tossed the book onto the bed.

"Ben said we should wake him up if we haven't found the book yet," Jason said.

"He's already awake, man. What exactly are we supposed to do with him?" Will asked.

"I'm going to assume Ben wants us to coax the answer out of him."

"And how do we do that?" Joy asked.

Will held up his knife. It gleamed in the dying rays of sunlight filtering into the room. "I think I have a couple of ideas."

* * *

JASON, WILL, JOY, AND GABRIELLE JOINED THE THREE witches downstairs.

"Are you sure you want to do this?" Jason said.

"Do what?" Jen asked.

Joy and Gabrielle took up a post to watch over Gerald. Jen, Lisa, and Daphne lowered their wands.

"We didn't find the book," Jason said. "It was a grimoire? I think that's what you guys call it."

"Great," Daphne said. "What should we do now?"

"Will has some ideas about that." Jason motioned for Will to share.

"Do you see this?" Will held up his knife. "This was made specifically for dispatching demons. It's the only thing I've ever come across that can cause them pain when they possess a body."

"Are you talking about torturing this creature?" Jen asked. She folded her arms across her chest. "I don't think I can stand by and watch that."

"I'm with Jen," Lisa said.

"Me, too," Daphne said. "It goes against everything we stand for."

"It wasn't that long ago, if I remember correctly, ladies, that y'all didn't have a problem torturing Gabriel Curtis in order to exorcise him."

"He was a serial killer. He had already murdered three girls and had another one stashed up in his attic," Lisa argued.

"This is completely different. Gerald did not ask to be possessed. Gabriel Curtis went looking for a demon to possess him," Jen said.

"Exactly. Just one monster looking for another. Either way, it's really not what we practice," Daphne said. "That kind of stuff taints your soul forever."

"All right then," Will began. "Perhaps you ladies should step outside. I don't have a problem doing this. That's not Gerald anymore. I know it's not what you want to hear. But once you get that demon out of him, he will never be the same. That is, assuming it doesn't kill him when he's exorcised," Will said.

Lisa put her hands on her hips. "Jason, I can't believe that you'd even entertain letting this happen."

"Technically, I don't have any authority here. And Will has a point. This guy is dead either way. If the demon doesn't kill him, it will leave him just an insane shell, from what Ben has said."

"I can't believe you're saying that," Lisa said. "Are you saying the ends justify the means?"

"If it helps us find that book and save Charlie, yes. Absolutely. Ben texted me. Charlie is deteriorating fast. We need to find that book as fast as we can to save her."

"Just so you know," Jen said, "Charlie is not gonna like it if you sacrifice Gerald to save her."

"I'll deal with that when she wakes up," Jason said. "At the moment, she's not here, and she doesn't get a say. Go ahead, Will. Do what you need to do.

"I'm not gonna stay here to watch it." Lisa started for the door. Joy stepped in front of her. "

"Lisa," Joy began. "I know this is disturbing. And I completely understand how you feel."

Lisa took a step back. "You do?"

"Yes, of course. Believe it or not, as reapers, we have nothing but the utmost respect for the human soul. And any suffering that one endures is difficult for us to watch as well. But... "

"But?" Lisa said.

"We need you. Torturing this man could enrage the demon inside him. And rage will only make him stronger. I implore you to stay. To help us keep him bound while Will questions him. Please." Joy held up her hands, her fingers laced together as if she were begging.

Lisa's shoulders sank with defeat, and she glanced up at the ceiling, her jaw tightening. She blew out a heavy breath and turned around. "Fine. I'll stay. But I want it on the record that it does not make me happy."

"So noted," Jason said. "For the record, I don't like it either. But Charlie's more important to me than this demon. And I'll do whatever it takes to save her."

"I'm with Lisa," Jen said. "I'll stay and help. But, trust me, I will be complaining loudly once Charlie is well."

"Me, too," Daphne said.

"I understand." Jason turned to Sabine and Marigold standing quietly on the sidelines. "What about you two?"

"It's not ideal," Marigold began. "Especially since it's wearing Gerald's face, but we know it's not Gerald."

"I agree with Marigold," Sabine said.

"Good," Jason said. "Let's get started."

The witches surrounded Gerald and held out their wands, ready to bind him up if he broke loose.

Will stepped up to the metal armchair where the demon's arms and legs had been bound by thin silvery beams of light. Will kicked the toe of his boot against Gerald's tennis shoe. "Wake up!

Gerald's head swayed back and forth on his chest. Will touched the knife to Gerald's hand. He did not slice or draw blood in any way, but the touch of the metal made Gerald scream. His head popped up, his eyes completely black. Rage molded every feature from his brow to his chin. His lips curled back in a snarl.

The demon struggled against the bindings, lifting the chair up an inch into the air.

"Dammit." Lisa pointed her wand at Gerald's feet, and the thin yellow light emitting from the tip bound his ankles. Daphne and Jen pointed their wands, each taking one of Gerald's hands. Yellow beams of light coiled around his wrists. Sabine used her wand to create an anchor of light that wrapped around the metal crossbar between the legs of the chair. She pulled back on her wand, and the chair set down on the floor again.

The demon snarled and shook his body the best that he could against his bindings. Sweat dripped from his scalp and spittle escaped from his mouth while he yelled, "I will take such great joy crushing your skull, human."

Will lifted the knife from the demon's skin. A red burn mark in the shape of the knife tip glowed a dark, angry red.

The demon sucked in air then hopped up and down trying to break free. Will moved up the creature's arm hovering the knife above the skin. Gerald's gaze followed the knife's tip. His breathing quickened when the knife passed his upper arm and Will hovered the gleaming metal near his head.

"Not my face, man. Come on. That will leave a scar on your good pal Gerald here forever," the demon argued.

"Good point," Will said. He quickly brought the knife to Gerald's arm, resting more of the blade on his forearm.

The demon roared. The chair moved an inch forward despite the anchor. "You can make all of this stop by just telling us where you hid the book."

"You'd have to ask Gerald. I have no idea where it is."

"I don't believe you," Will said. He pressed the knife harder into the skin of the forearm. A thin line of blood drew forth and dripped, mixing with the sweat on Gerald's arm.

Jason reached up to stop Will. The whole thing turned his stomach. And Daphne was right. Charlie would be disgusted if she ever found out about this.

The loud diesel engine pulling into the driveway delivered a welcome sound. Will lifted the knife from Gerald's forearm. Another burn mark appeared, followed by blisters. The long slice of a wound dripped blood onto the carpet below.

"Hang tight. Maybe that's the transport." Jason turned his back and headed toward the door. Behind him, Jason heard a great crash and he froze in his tracks. Gerald's body seized, and he shook his head, whipping back and forth. Jason rejoined the circle in time to see Gerald's eyes roll back in his head, showing only the whites. His body tensed, his hands digging into the metal arms of the chair so hard that his fingernails broke. Then his whole body went limp. His head tipped forward, and his chin rested on his chest.

"I told you this was a bad idea," Lisa said. "Joy, check his pulse. Make sure he's still breathing.

Joy nodded and pressed two fingers against Gerald's neck. "There's definitely a heartbeat. It's surprisingly strong."

Gerald moaned and brought his chin up. His eyes widened when he scanned the faces standing around him. No traces of the demon's black eyes remained.

"Where am I?" Who are you?" Gerald looked around at all the faces with a wild look in his eyes.

"Marigold? Sabine?" Gerald said. The two witches moved in closer.

"You know us?" Marigold said warily.

"Of course I know you," Gerald said, indignant. He looked around. "This is my house. How did we get to my house?"

"Gerald, you've been possessed." Marigold knelt in front of him and took his hand in hers.

"Possessed." Gerald shook his head. "No, that can't be."

"I'm sorry, but it's true," Marigold said. "I need you to think hard for me, Gerald. You took something from Lauren's office, remember?"

Gerald squeezed his eyes shut. Tears flowed from the corners of his closed lids, melting into the sweat on his face. His body shook as he cried. A horrible sob escaped him. "I... I hit Lauren."

"No, Gerald, that wasn't you. That was the thing inside you. Where is that thing?"

"I don't know. It comes and goes," Gerald said. "But sometimes... I can still see what it's making me do."

"I know," Marigold whispered.

"Enough!" Gabrielle moved in close to Gerald. "I have had enough." Gabrielle shed her glamour the way a snake would shed its skin. Once free of the human mask, Gabrielle flitted around Gerald.

"Tell me where my book is, human. Tell me now. I know you saw where the demon hid it."

Gerald began to cry again. His shoulders shook, and a bone-chilling moan escaped his lips.

"I killed that man," Gerald wept. "I killed that man and his whole family."

"No," Jason said. He knelt next to Gerald. "The demon did that."

"It's all jumbled up in my head. I remember it all. But it's in bits and pieces like a puzzle," Gerald said. "I can still hear him. He's still inside me, breathing like a sleeping dragon."

"It's okay, Gerald," Sabine said. "We're going to get you out of here. And we're going to get you some help."

"You should just kill me now," Gerald said. "There is no coming back from this. I can hear him whispering and whispering."

"What is he whispering?" Jason asked.

"He's telling me to kill you all. And then to kill myself. He's right. I don't deserve to live. I killed that man and his wife... " Gerald's mouth opened with a silent scream. Finally, he choked out, "I killed those children. How could I do that?"

"Gerald, please let us help you," Sabine implored.

Gerald wept harder, unable to articulate any words, making only unintelligible noises.

"If you saw what the demon made you do, did you also see where he hid my book?" Gabrielle asked, her voice silky and strange.

"I saw... " Gerald stuttered out the words. "I saw... " His body shook with such violence Jason thought he might hurt himself. "Oh goddess." Gerald twitched from head to toe. "Can't breathe."

"Let him loose," Jason said.

"Wait, I thought—" Will began.

"Let him loose! He's having some sort of seizure." Jason placed himself behind Gerald and held the seizing man's head so that he wouldn't snap his own neck.

"This is a bad idea," Sabine said. "That thing is still inside him."

"It won't be for long if he kills himself, now, will he?" Jason said.

"Actually, demons have been known to occupy dead bodies for months," Marigold chimed in.

"I don't care. Y'all are the ones that wanted to keep

him alive. Now let him go before he bites his damned tongue off!" Jason said.

"Okay, okay," Marigold said. "Let him go."

Gerald fell forward onto the ground and continued flailing. Jason rolled him over onto his back and pinned his shoulder to the floor with his knee and held the man's hand.

"Help me hold him down."

Lisa took one leg; Jen took the other. Marigold took Gerald's other hand.

"It's okay, Gerald," Jason said. "You're okay."

After a moment or two, Gerald stopped thrashing. His body stilled, and his breathing evened out.

Gerald's eyes fluttered open, and he looked into Jason's face. "It's in the vault."

"The book?" Jason asked.

"The vault... " Gerald squeezed Jason's hand so tightly he thought it might break. Gerald grimaced with pain. "Can't... Breathe. Can't... "

Gerald pressed his hand to the center of his chest. "Hurts."

"Oh, my Goddess. Is he having a heart attack?" Sabine asked.

"Jen, go upstairs and check his meds. See if there's any aspirin," Jason said. "I need to call 911."

"No!" Sabine said. "You can't do that."

"Are you crazy? We have to help him," Jason snapped.

"You think I don't know that," Sabine snapped. "We need to take him to the DOL Medical Center. We have the transport."

"That's over an hour away," Jason said.

"Jason's right," Lisa said. "We need to take him to the nearest hospital."

"Y'all." Daphne's voice was weak. "Y'all, I think he's dead."

"What?" Jason looked down at Gerald. His hand had fallen away from his chest, and there was no more pain on his face. Jason pressed his fingers against Gerald's neck. He could find no pulse.

"Lisa call 911. I'm gonna start CPR." Jason tipped Gerald's head back, cleared his airway, and blew into his mouth before he moved to chest compressions. *15 compressions and then a breath. 15 compressions and then a breath. 15 compressions and then a breath.* It had been a while since he'd had to perform CPR. He'd forgotten how strenuous it could be.

15 compressions and a breath.

A sharp pain radiated through his lip, and he jerked his head away from Gerald's mouth. His lip tore, and the salty, coppery taste of blood filled his mouth. Jason pressed his fingers against his swelling lip.

"What the fuck?" He looked down, and Gerald's eyes were open, but they were completely black. Jason scrambled backward, dragging Lisa along with him. Sabine jumped back, and Daphne fell on her behind. The demon sat up straight, with no doubt who he was now. There was nothing left of Gerald.

Gabrielle swirled around the group before she stopped and hovered in front of the demon. "Where is my book, demon?"

The demon answered her with a laugh. "You will never know, reaper. And your friend will die."

"You have done enough damage." Gabrielle stood tall. Her reaper robes, dark and silky, flowed around her. In one bony hand, she held her scythe. The demon rose to his feet, ready to fight. She reared the scythe backward and charged forward.

The two supernatural creatures tangled up for a moment, and Jason couldn't tell where she began, and the demon ended. He motioned for Lisa and Daphne to head to the door. Jen descended the stairs with a bottle of aspirin in one hand and a bottle of medication in the other.

"Come on, Jen. We have to get out of here." Jason waved her down from the steps and onto the front porch. When the large denim couch flew across the room, Joy made her way along the walls, trying to avoid contact with the two battling creatures.

"Shouldn't you intervene?" Jason asked.

"This is not my fight," Joy said.

A lamp shattered against a wall near their heads.

Jason ushered Joy out the door. A guttural cry stopped him in his tracks, and he threw a glance over his shoulder, aware that the reaper had sunk her scythe into Gerald's chest. She spun around with a smoky black shadow caught on her blade. Gerald's body crumpled to the floor. Gabrielle continued to spin and spin, so fast she was nothing but a blur. Then she disappeared, taking the demon with her.

CHAPTER 25

The last person Charlie expected to see on her beach was Gerald Handley. He looked so different than she remembered. Handsome. A little thinner and no gray in his hair. His dark brown skin glowed with a youthfulness Charlie had never seen before, and he had no trace of stress anywhere in his energy. But of course, what did she expect? This was the afterlife, wasn't it? She hadn't looked in a mirror since arriving, but she guessed that if she did, she might see a younger, prettier version of herself. Charlie raised her arm and waved. Gerald grinned from ear to ear and sped up.

"I wasn't really expecting to see you here today, Gerald," Charlie said. "Or are you just a figment of my imagination?"

"Naw, no ma'am. I am not a figment of your imagination. I'm really here. And from what I was told, I could stop by here and say hello before moving on to my own afterlife," Gerald said.

"That's wonderful. It's always nice to have visitors. But why would you want to stop here?" Charlie asked.

"I have some information for you," Gerald said. "I was trying to tell that young man. That deputy sheriff friend of yours."

"Jason?" Charlie asked, shocked that Gerald had seen Jason again.

"Yes, ma'am. He was with me in my last moments. Held my hand and everything. Turns out he's actually a good guy," Gerald said.

"Yes, he is," Charlie agreed.

"He kept tell me it's going to be okay." Gerald's expression became dreamy, and he let his gaze settle on the horizon. "And I guess he was right."

"If you're here, that means you're not there anymore," Charlie muttered.

"Yeah. My old ticker just couldn't take it anymore. I was already on pills for my heart. I've had angina for years, and my last moments were... " Gerald spoke with a thoughtful expression. "Let's just say my last moments were the most stressful I think I've ever had."

"I'm so sorry to hear that," Charlie said. "You're okay

now, though. I mean, you're here." She gestured to the beautiful beach stretching all around them.

"I am." He nodded and smiled.

"So, what message did you have for me from Jason?"

"There's a book. You probably remember it. It belonged to a reaper. Anyway, long story short, Lauren stole it from the clean room. And I was, well let's just say, I was commandeered against my will."

"You were possessed?"

"Yes. I'm afraid so. Anyway, in a moment of lucidity, I took the book and hid it away while that monster slept inside me."

"How did you do that?" She moved closer to hear every word. "I mean, without the demon inside you seeing it happen?"

"Well, it turns out that demons sometimes like to sleep when they're inside a person, and I sensed when he'd fallen unconscious. I remembered a few things I'd learned a long time ago when I first started at the DOL and read up on different ways to rid yourself of a demon—"

"Did you find any?"

"I found a few things. Turns out a concoction of bourbon and Fumaria will actually put a demon into a deep sleep."

"I had no idea," Charlie said.

"You'll learn all about it eventually. Although, I'm not

sure it's still part of the training curriculum for new hires."

"I'm not sure I follow. Why would I learn it?" Charlie held her hand up and gestured to her surroundings. "Why would I ever leave here?"

"Because this isn't where you belong. Not yet, Miss Charlie," Gerald said. "Can't you feel that humming?"

Charlie dug her toes into the sand. "Every once in a while, there's this dissonant note that plays. It makes me want to put my hands over my ears."

"It's just a quiet drone but it's enough to drive a person crazy if they had to listen to it long enough," Gerald said. "This isn't my afterlife, and I hear it good in here."

"Yes, I hear it, too. But I just haven't been sure about what it means."

"Now, I'm no expert. I just got here myself. But seems like you're out of harmony with this environment. I think that's why I'm hearing it here. I don't think that's the way it should be."

"No, I suppose it's not," Charlie said softly. "Gerald, what was the message?"

"Oh right. Sorry. The book is in the vault."

"The book is in the vault. What vault?" Charlie asked.

"I have a vault in the floor of my boat house. A place where I store some of my private papers."

Charlie nodded, listening carefully.

"I stuck it in there. It's out of the way, and the vault is climate controlled to protect whatever's in there."

"Okay." Charlie shrugged. "I still don't understand how I'm going to find it from here."

"You're going back."

"But—"

"Repeat after me, Miss Charlie. It's in the vault in Gerald's boathouse."

"Gerald. Really. This is ridic—"

"Just humor me. If you don't go back, then there's no harm in at least committing it to memory for now."

Charlie crossed her arms. "Fine."

"Good. Now repeat after me. It's in the vault in Gerald's boathouse."

"It's in the vault in Gerald's boathouse," Charlie repeated.

"Very good. Now you just keep saying that over and over again. And Miss Charlie, don't forget, you still have a son to raise who needs some instruction on how to handle those natural abilities of his." Gerald tapped the side of his nose and cocked his head as if listening to something. "It's time for me to move on to my afterlife."

"Okay," Charlie said and smiled. "It's in the vault in Gerald's boathouse."

Gerald gave her a quick nod and began to turn away. Then he paused and looked back. "It's been lovely knowing you, Miss Charlie. Now, it's time for you to get back in your body. You've got a lot of work to do."

"I wish it was that simple," Charlie said.

"It is," Gerald said. "You just have to follow that note out."

"How do I do that?" Charlie asked.

"Just close your eyes," Gerald said. "It will take you where you need to go."

"Right, but how do you know?" Charlie asked, taking a step toward him. The waves lapped gently against the shore in a soothing rhythm, but for the first time since arriving, Charlie felt anything but soothed.

"I just know is all. When it's your time to be here, you'll know, too. You take care, Miss Charlie, and close your eyes!"

Gerald gave her a short wave, turned, and took a few steps before he faded away.

"It's in the vault in Gerald's boathouse," Charlie muttered. She turned her back on the ocean and closed her eyes.

* * *

CHARLIE'S EYES FLEW OPEN, AND SHE SAT UP STRAIGHT IN bed. Sensors around her began to beep wildly, and something metal clattered to the floor.

"It's in the vault in Gerald's boathouse," Charlie

shouted. Tomeka jumped up from her seat next to Charlie's bed.

"You're okay, Charlie," Tomeka said. "You need to lie back down."

Charlie grabbed onto Tomeka's hand and yanked her down close. "You have to find it. It's in the lost and found vault."

"It's okay," Tomeka said. "You're going to be okay."

"You're not listening to me." Charlie's teeth chattered from the cold filling every space in her body. "Tell Ben. The book is in the vault in Gerald's boat house."

A nurse rushed in and looked at the monitors before she pulled a syringe out of her pocket and plunged the needle into the input port on the IV bag.

Charlie's teeth slowly stopped chattering, and she fell back onto her bed. The cold penetrated her whole being.

"Tell them to check the vault," she whispered. She fought the panic threatening to wrap its hands around her throat, threatening to cut off her air. Her arm and shoulder ached so badly, but all she could think of was finding the vault and the book inside.

"Darius, go get Ben," Tomeka commanded. "But before you go, calm her down first."

"Sure thing," Darius said. He placed his hand on Charlie's forearm. "Breathe in for me, Charlie. Take a deep breath." His chest puffed out, and Charlie mimicked him. Her lungs expanded, and the panic receded some.

"Good job. You keep breathing. I'm going to go get Ben."

Charlie's nostrils flared out, and she pulled in as much air as she could.

A few moments later, Ben appeared with a doctor in tow. Charlie tried to get off her bed.

"Ben, we have to go to Gerald's boathouse."

"Whoa, whoa, whoa." The doctor rushed to the bedside and held Charlie in place. "Not yet, Ms. Payne. Not yet."

"Ben," Charlie said, desperation dancing on her nerves. "Ben, please."

"Charlie, please get back in bed," Ben said. Charlie reached for his hand and he took it.

"The book is in the vault in Gerald's boathouse." Charlie pulled on his arm, trying to draw him closer. She'd never felt so desperate before. Why wasn't he getting it?

"How do you know that?"

"I..." She blinked, trying call up the specific memory, but it was all hazy. She remembered Gerald's face. His kind smile.

"I don't know. I can't remember exactly. I just know the book is in the vault in Gerald's boathouse. Please. Please believe me."

"I believe you," Ben said. He squeezed her hand. "You rest now, okay? We're going to check it out."

"Promise?" Charlie asked.

"Promise," Ben said.

Charlie let out a strained breath and let her head rest on the pillow again. "Good."

Her eyelids closed slowly. All she wanted to do now was sleep.

CHAPTER 26

J ason, Lisa, and Sabine stalked across the dark backyard to the small boathouse overlooking Gerald's little corner of the lake. The light from their flashlights bounced on the ground ahead of them, leading the way.

Jen, Daphne, Joy, and Marigold concentrated their efforts on combing the back yard, garage, and edge of the woods hoping to find the bodies of the Cochrans. Gerald had admitted to killing them. He must have put them somewhere, and in Jason's mind, the easiest way to dispose of them would be to bury them somewhere on the property.

When they got to the heavy steel door of the boathouse, they found it padlocked. Jason lifted the lock and inspected it.

"I've got some bolt cutters in my trunk," Jason said.

"No need," Sabine said. She stepped in front of him and took the lock in her hand. She whispered a quick incantation, and the locking mechanism clicked, releasing the shank. Sabine lifted the padlock from the metal loop and opened the door. "There ya go."

"Well, that's handy," Jason muttered, and entered the boathouse. He flashed the beam of his small flashlight around the perimeter of the room. It landed first on a large chest freezer and then on a large black safe bolted to the floor in the corner of the room.

"There it is." He looked to Sabine and pointed his light at the safe. "You think that thing you did to get us in here will work on that?"

Sabine grinned. "Of course. Hopefully, he hasn't put any curses or counter spells on it to keep someone from opening it."

"Yeah, let's hope," Jason said.

"Don't worry. I'm very skilled at this," Sabine said. "I can get around most deterrents. The only exception might be a death curse, but knowing Gerald, it probably won't be something so horrible."

"Great," Jason said. He stood back to let her work. The bright white of the freezer kept drawing his eye to it. Maybe he'd been a cop too long, but something told him to look inside. He walked over to it, and a cold shiver skittered across his back when he saw the brand new padlock.

"Shit," he muttered. Lisa drew up next to him.

"What is it?" Lisa asked.

Sabine turned the lock of the safe, and it clicked. She pushed the lever and opened the door. "See I told you. Easy peasy." She flashed her light at the freezer, and the shiny padlock glowed in the darkness. "Why would you put a lock on a freezer?"

"Not for any good reason I know of," Jason said. "Would you mind?"

"Of course not," Sabine said. She made quick work of unlocking the padlock and stepped back, an anxious look on her face.

"You might want to step back too, hon," Jason said.

Lisa nodded and joined Sabine a few feet away. Jason took a quick breath and held it before he jerked the freezer door open. The sight of the frozen bodies, carefully wrapped up in plastic, turned his stomach.

"What is it?" Sabine asked. She took a step closer.

"No," Jason held up a hand. "Y'all just stay there. I think it's the family y'all were searching for."

"Oh, sweet goddess." Sabine moved next to him. "Oh, my gosh. That poor family."

Jason closed the freezer door and pulled his phone from his pocket.

"Who are you calling?" Sabine asked.

"I need to call this in to the local authorities," Jason said.

"No, you can't do that. This is a witch matter and our dominion. The local authorities handed it over to us. We'll handle it," Sabine said. "I'll get a team out here to take care of everything."

"Just like that?" Jason asked.

"Yes," Sabine said. "Just like that. Now we need to get that reaper Joy down here to handle this book and get it back to the DOL as quickly as possible to take care of Charlie. Unless you'd rather help me deal with these bodies?"

"Uh... no." Jason said. "It's your jurisdiction."

"What are we waiting for?" Lisa snapped. "Let's get this book back to the DOL Medical Center."

CHARLIE'S EYES FLUTTERED OPEN, AND SHE SQUEEZED something rough in her hand. She held up the small linen bag. Where had that come from? She shifted her gaze to the chair in the corner where her son slept curled up in a small recliner. Her ex-husband Scott sat in an uncomfortable-looking plastic and metal chair with his hands folded across his chest. His head leaned back against the wall with his eyes closed. A familiar snore escaped his partly open mouth. She smiled and let her gaze drift around the room until it landed on Tom staring out the small window.

"Tom?" Charlie said, her voice a little froggy.

Tom jumped a little as if he'd been goosed. A moment later, he was at her bedside, taking her hand into his. "You're awake. Finally."

"Finally," she repeated. "What day is it?"

"Sunday."

She looked past Tom to Evan. "Did he have his game?"

Tom glanced over his shoulder and nodded. "Why don't you ask him? Evan."

"No, it's okay, let him sleep."

Evan roused at the sound of his name, and he sat up on the edge of his seat, rubbing his eyes. "Mom? Are you awake?"

Charlie smiled. "I am." She felt around for the bed controller, and when she found it, lifted the head of her bed to a more comfortable position. Scott made a snorting noise and started awake.

"What? What's going on?" Scott said, sitting up straight in his chair.

"Mom's awake," Evan said. He stood up and moved to the other side of her bed and sat down. He reached for the mojo bag in her hand. "It worked."

"That's yours?" Charlie asked.

"Yep."

"Did Evangeline help you make that?" Charlie asked.

"No. A witch named Magda did," Evan said. He tucked the bag back into Charlie's hand.

"Magda?" Charlie looked to Tom, and he shrugged and shook his head as if the news was as much a surprise to him as it was to her. "Sounds like we have a lot to talk about."

Evan gave her a nonchalant shrug. "Not that much."

Scott pointed to the door. "I'm gonna step out and let the others know you're awake."

"Thank you, Scott," Charlie said. Scott ducked out of the room. "Sounds like I've got a lot to talk about with him, too."

"Not that much." Tom grinned. "How are you feeling?"

"I'm okay." She held up her arm. "I'm not in pain anymore."

"Good," Tom said.

"Hey." Charlie shifted her attention to Evan. "Did you win your game? I'm assuming that's what this is for." She held up the mojo bag.

"I didn't go, but Connor texted me. We lost. In a big way." Evan played with a frayed edge of her blanket, a strange smile on his lips.

"I'm sorry, honey," Charlie said, touching his hand. He grabbed onto her hand and held it tight.

"It's just a stupid game, Mom. It's not important," he said.

"Come here." She pulled him to her. "Give your old mom a hug."

"Sure," he said and cuddled up with her. She kissed the top of his head, and a bittersweet pang filled her chest.

CHARLIE STOOD ON THE BACK PORCH OF HER UNCLE'S HOUSE watching her cousin Jen prepare the back yard for the solstice bonfire and celebration. Jen ordered Ruby, Evan, and his friend Rachel around like a pro, telling them which chairs to put where and how to set up the table for their family ritual.

Tom stepped on to the porch and sidled up to her, putting his arm around her waist, and handing her a cup of Evangeline's hot apple cider. The warm mug felt good in her hand, and she blew on the hot sweet liquid before taking a sip. At least the weather had turned cool, and the skies were clear. It would be a lovely night for welcoming back the sun.

Tom leaned over and kissed her on the temple. "Are you okay?"

"I'm alive, and I'm here with the people I love the

most, so I'm good. How about you? Any news from our friend, Gabrielle?"

"As a matter of fact, she did as you asked, mainly because I think she felt a debt of gratitude that we found her book," Tom said.

"Well, don't keep me in suspense. What did she find out?"

"She found the demon, K'Ozra was what she called him, and with a little coaxing, he told her that Gerald Handley had encountered John Cochran hanging around the DOL parking structure. The possessed John attacked Gerald, and when they fought, K'Ozra told Gabrielle that he jumped into Gerald's body because he was alive and could get him into the DOL without casting suspicion. K'Ozra had killed Cochran when the man summoned him, and then possessed his body."

"And his family?"

"K'Ozra actually killed them and kept them in a minivan he'd stolen," Tom said.

"That's terrible." Charlie shook her head and took another sip of her cider. "This whole case has just been one horrible tragedy after another."

"Are you having second thoughts about going back after the holiday?" Tom asked.

Charlie opened her mouth to answer, but a chuckle escaped her lips instead. She shook her head. "No. No, I think I'm where I'm supposed to be. There's still a lot of good I can do."

Tom squeezed her waist tighter. "Yes, there certainly is."

"Will you tell Gabrielle thank you for me?"

"Of course," Tom said.

Jen walked over to the steps and put her hands on her hips. "Are y'all just going to stand there all day or are you going to help?"

Charlie put her cup on the top of the porch railing. "We're coming. Good goddess, you'd think almost dying would give a girl a pass on this sort of thing." Charlie muttered as she descended the stairs.

"Not today, Charlie Payne. Not today," Jen said.

THANK YOU FOR READING *NATURAL BORN WITCH*. I KNEW this story was going to be a challenge because it took Charlie to new places, with lots of new faces and friends to be made. So many of you have reached out to me over the course of the series and asked about Evan, and this book felt like the right place to introduce him, his abilities and how much of a journey he has before him so I'm excited about all the possibilities for Evan in future books.

In the next book, *Bad Omens*, Charlie stumbles across

an old family secret that sets her on the path to determine whether her parents and her aunt Ellen, Jen and Lisa's mother, were murdered. There will be lots of mystery, intrigue, ghostly encounters and family time to keep you entertained.

Sign up here to be notified when *Bad Omens* is available for preorder or has launched, http://eepurl.com/c7-jIL

CONNECT WITH ME

One of the things I love most about writing is building a relationship with my readers. We can connect in several different ways.

JOIN MY READER'S NEWSLETTER.

By signing up for my newsletter, you will get information on preorders, new releases and exclusive content just for my reader's newsletter. You can join by clicking here: http://eepurl.com/c7-jIL

You can also follow me on my Amazon page if you prefer not to get another email in your inbox. Follow me here.

CONNECT WITH ME ON FACEBOOK

Want to comment on your favorite scene? Or make suggestions for a funny ghostly encounter for Charlie? Or tell me what sort of magic you'd like to see Jen, Daphne and Lisa perform? Like my Facebook page and let me know. I post content there regularly and talk with my readers every day.

FACEBOOK: HTTPS://WWW. facebook.com/wendywangauthor

LET'S TALK ABOUT OUR FAVORITE BOOKS IN MY READERS group on Facebook.

Readers   Group: https://www.facebook.com/ groups/1287348628022940/ ;

YOU CAN ALWAYS DROP ME AN EMAIL. I LOVE TO HEAR FROM my readers

Email: http://www. wendywangbooks.com/contact.html

THANK YOU AGAIN FOR READING!

Made in the USA
Coppell, TX
23 May 2020